MAR 19

D0866804

ADVANCE PRAISE FOR
THE MANIC PIXIE DREAM BOY IMPROVEMENT PROJECT

"How long has it been since you had a good laugh? This book is the one you've been waiting for. Witty, sharp, surprising—a refreshing read."

—Martha Brockenbrough, author of
The Game of Love and Death

"Funny, romantic, and delightfully meta—*The Manic Pixie Dream Boy Improvement Project* was a joy to read from beginning to end."

—Jess Rothenberg, author of
The Catastrophic History of You & Me and *The Kingdom*

The MANIC PiXIE DREAM BOY IMPROVEMENT Project

LENORE APPELHANS

carolrhoda LAB

MINNEAPOLIS

Text copyright © 2019 by Lenore Appelhans

Carolrhoda Lab™ is a trademark of Lerner Publishing Group, Inc.

All rights reserved. International copyright secured. No part of this book may be reproduced, stored in a retrieval system, or transmitted in any form or by any means—electronic, mechanical, photocopying, recording, or otherwise—without the prior written permission of Lerner Publishing Group, Inc., except for the inclusion of brief quotations in an acknowledged review.

Carolrhoda Lab™
An imprint of Carolrhoda Books
A division of Lerner Publishing Group, Inc.
241 First Avenue North
Minneapolis, MN 55401 USA

For reading levels and more information, look up this title at
www.lernerbooks.com.

Title font: 9george/Shutterstock.com.
Map © Laura Westlund/Indepenent Picture Service.

Main body text set in Janson Text LT Std 10.5/15.
Typeface provided by Linotype AG.

Library of Congress Cataloging-in-Publication Data

Names: Appelhans, Lenore, author.
Title: The Manic Pixie Dream Boy Improvement Project / by Lenore Appelhans.
Description: Minneapolis, MN : Carolrhoda Lab, [2019] | Summary: "Riley, a Manic Pixie Dream Boy, lives in TropeTown, where he makes a living appearing as a side character in novels—until he and his fellow manic pixies must ban together to save themselves from retirement" —Provided by publisher.
Identifiers: LCCN 2018010972 (print) | LCCN 2018018162 (ebook) | ISBN 9781541541849 (eb pdf) | ISBN 9781541512597 (th : alk. paper)
Subjects: | CYAC: Characters in literature—Fiction. | Insurgency—Fiction. | Books and reading—Fiction. | Friendship—Fiction.
Classification: LCC PZ7.A6447 (ebook) | LCC PZ7.A6447 Man 2019 (print) | DDC [Fic]—dc23

LC record available at https://lccn.loc.gov/2018010972

Manufactured in the United States of America
1-44012-34122-10/19/2018

For M.W.E.
I'll always be by your side.

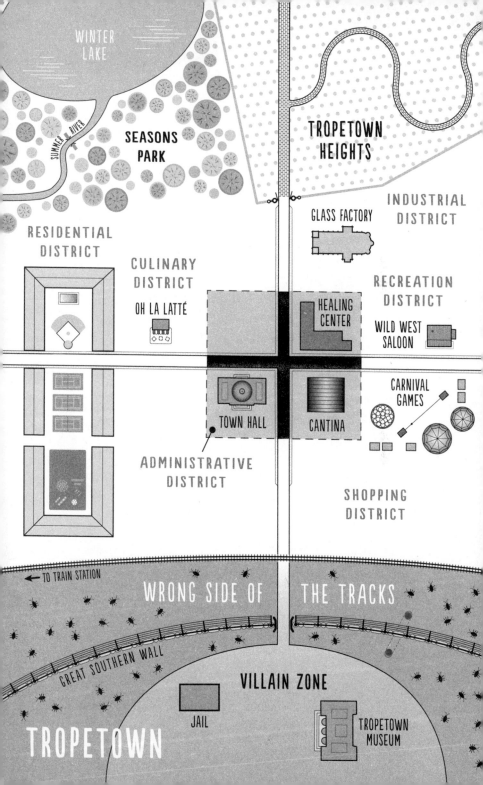

Dear Riley (Manic Pixie Dream Boy #0002),

An Author alleged you went off script on your last completed project, your second such infraction. Statute 124 of the TropeTown Code of Conduct mandates compulsory behavioral therapy in a group environment. Please report to Room 9393 of the Healing Center at 8:00 a.m. daily, starting tomorrow, for the following eight weeks. We encourage you to take this chance at rehabilitation seriously. As you are aware, should your behavior warrant a third complaint, a disciplinary tribunal will convene to discuss your possible termination.

Sincerely,
Your Friendly TropeTown Council

CHAPTER 1

I crumple the notice in my fist and hurl it into the recycling chute. I guess I suspected this might happen. I tried my best on my last project, but my Author gave me so much hassle.

There'd be days on end where I wouldn't be called into work at all, and then—boom—like, three furious all-nighters in a row. I could have put in a complaint about poor working conditions, but being agreeable is characteristic of my Trope, so I didn't. And now I'm in danger of termination.

Termination. That's a scary word. No one really knows what happens to you when you're terminated. You board a train on the outskirts of town. The train always comes back empty. There are rumors that termination means getting thrown into a shredder and having your traits sorted through to recycle into new stock characters. Even though I'm fictional, I'd prefer to stay whole.

Anyway, as much as I'd love to indignantly ignore the Council's mandate, I can't. First of all, there's that whole agreeable characteristic I mentioned. And second, I get the feeling the Council keeps close tabs on me—on all of us. I don't know exactly how, or to what extent, but I've run into several Wild Conspiracy Theorists who are convinced the whole town is crawling with hidden cameras and bugs. I need to err on the side of being a model TropeTown citizen to get back in the Council's good graces.

I walk outside and shield my eyes from the bright sun until they adjust. It's always sunny in TropeTown. Oversaturated blue sky and green grass make it seem like we're living in a cartoon. Perfect, puffy white clouds float above me. Fresh and calibrated air ensures we neither shiver nor sweat while in the city environs. At this time of morning, the Service Industry Tropes hustle to their employment stations, and Leisure Tropes clog the wide, tree-lined avenue running east-west in front of the residential complex where I live.

All around me, birds chirp and children laugh, and I envy their carefree happiness. Clearly they did not receive a morale-leeching summons to therapy.

I glance down at my TropeTown employee band. It's not likely to light up today with an Author summons, as I recently finished work on my last novel and haven't started a new project yet.

That's just as well—I'd like to be alone while I contemplate this setback. I tap the pocket of my jacket to confirm I have a full packet of crackers, and I head to my favorite place in TropeTown, the wooden bridge that crosses Summer River in Seasons Park.

I hate that I don't feel up to greeting people with my usual pep, so I keep my head down and walk as quickly as I can, blocking out my surroundings and repeating positivity mantras to myself—something my best friend and mentor, Finn, taught me to do. Everything will be okay. Everything will be better than okay. Everything will work out for the best, even if I can't see how right now.

By the time I reach the bridge, I'm already more hopeful. I take out a handful of crackers and crush them. The ducks respond to my crackling and crunching, swimming my way with eager beaks. I toss the crumbs into the air, and they hit the water like confetti. Frenzied quacking ensues. Other than that, peace reigns.

So I'm slightly annoyed when a clomping sound alerts me to the presence of another human. When I turn, my annoyance fades into concern as a teetering tower of books with legs walks toward me. Sexy legs clad in daisy-printed leggings. I have a vision of pages sinking down, down, down into an aquatic grave, bloating and warping all those beautiful words. I rush over to offer my help.

"Hey," I say.

She yelps and stumbles, and the books fall in a pile at her feet. We both bend down and reach for the same book at the same time. Our fingers brush, and I'm so startled by the electric reaction it creates that I look up.

I'm staring at her, and she's staring back at me through eyeglasses with heavy brown frames. Neither of us moves, except to grip the book even tighter.

The girl's wild, dark hair frames high cheekbones and red lips that seem set in a permanent smirk. She's a stranger, and yet familiar. I've never felt this kind of instant attraction to anyone before, and it literally takes my breath away. The moment stretches out between us, intense and full of meaning.

I exhale. She exhales.

I notice the title of the book we're both still clutching. *Pinocchio*. It must be a sign.

"This is my favorite novel," I say, giddy at the coincidence. She quirks an eyebrow. "Mine too."

I nod like I knew this already, because on some level, I did. "I'm Riley. Manic Pixie Dream Boy, at your service." I finally let go of the book.

"Zelda. Manic Pixie Dream Girl." Figures she'd be just my Trope. And by the looks of her, she's the Geek Chick subtype, the most cynical and most prone to actually getting her Trope inverted. I haven't spent much time around other Manic Pixies—except for Finn—but I know a lot about them thanks to the *TropeTown Guide to Character Types* every Trope comes with, standard issue.

She hugs *Pinocchio* to her chest. She wears a yellow T-shirt with a black outline of a square on it.

"Does the empty square mean something?" I ask.

"In the dozens of times I've worn this, no one has ever asked me that." She sounds pleased yet still guarded. "It's a periodic table square, and it's empty because I haven't found my element yet."

"May I suggest copper and tellurium?" I say before I can stop myself. "Because you're Cu-Te."

"O-MG." She laughs and her whole face lights up, her delight overpowering her jaded cool for a glorious moment.

We gather up the other titles and put them in two stacks, because of course I'll carry half of them to wherever she wants to take them. Based on her selections, I can tell she has eclectic taste—everything from superhero graphic novels to classics to guides about fixing up old toasters.

When we finish, I throw my remaining crackers to our large audience of waterfowl and pick up one of the piles. "Where to?"

Zelda winks. "Wandering about until we end up where we end up, of course."

"Makes perfect sense." Or it might if we weren't lugging

pounds of books around, but I'm not really programmed to voice anything so practical aloud.

As we walk across a vast field of emerald grass, I sneak glances at Zelda, who sneaks glances at me.

Even though I'll have access to her character trait sheet in the *TropeTown Guide* when I get home, there are a zillion little things I want to ask her. I can't settle on a single question, because as soon as it forms on my tongue, it suddenly seems too banal. I usually have no problem with amiable chatter, but I don't want to mess up with this girl. She throws me off-kilter in the most dizzying way.

Zelda breaks our silence with an exuberant shriek. "It's our lucky day!" We've wandered into a clover patch. She sits carefully, steadying the books and letting them rest in her lap, and she motions for me to do the same, so of course I do.

She plucks a pair of four-leaf clovers and presses the long stems between her fingers. She leans toward me, biting her lower lip while she arranges one of the clovers behind my ear. She puts the other in my open palm and twists her neck so I have better access to her ear. I let the leaves graze her cheek before I set the clover in place, and she closes her eyes and sighs.

Normally, I might ask if this is an invitation to kiss her, but the books form an awkward barrier between us, and also we've just met, and I fritter away so much time flip-flopping between my need to be a gentleman and my desire to be as close as possible to Zelda that her eyes pop open. She stands up with a frown. Am I a massive disappointment?

She leads me to the edge of the tree line of the Autumn Woods, a part of the park continually aglow with burnished reds, oranges, and golds. Dried leaves crunch and twigs crack under our feet. The humming of cicadas harmonizes with the chattering of birds and makes me ache with nostalgia for a childhood I never had.

We stop where the sunlight dapples her exposed collarbones. A breeze picks up, bringing a chill with it that sets goose bumps galloping across my skin.

"Please put them there," she instructs, indicating the flat top of a tree stump. Its surface reveals many rings, all fat with prosperity. Even though it never actually rains in TropeTown, all the flora and fauna thrive. It's one of the great mysteries of this place that sets it apart from Reader World. "My destination is close by, so . . ." She drags a toe of her shiny, yellow ankle boot in the dirt and doesn't look at me. Everything seemed to be going so well. What happened?

"Are you sure you don't still need help carrying them to wherever you were headed before you met me?" I ask, hoping to spend more time with her. "We could read aloud to each other from *Pinocchio*."

"That does sound fun." She looks around cautiously, as if to ascertain whether we're being watched, before whispering, "Can I trust you?"

"I would have to say yes. But should you really trust a guy who insists you can trust him?" I joke. She rewards me with her joyous laugh again. I could get addicted to her laugh.

She punches me softly on the shoulder. "You have a point there, bucko. But how about this? I'll be at the Ooh La Latte Café at seven tomorrow morning. I make it a priority to try a different flavor of tea each time I go."

Do I hear a choir singing? *She wants to see me again.* And I'll have just enough time to stop by the café before I have to be at therapy.

I grin and return her punch, trying to act super casual. "Maybe I'll see you there, then."

I have to force myself to turn and walk away. It's one of the hardest things I've ever done. But it's also the happiest I've been since Finn disappeared a few months ago. Suddenly the Council's letter doesn't bother me as much.

CHAPTER 2

Now, I bet you have a lot of questions. About where I come from and what my purpose is and who I really am inside. I have those same questions.

You want an origin story. Fine. Our Council founded TropeTown to be a repository for commonly recurring literary devices, situations, and characters in creative works. So I appeared here one day a few years ago, fully formed. Was I created, or did I spring spontaneously into existence because of Reader World's need for my type? The fact I came with a character trait sheet *seems* to point to intelligent design, but I don't actually know.

And now that I've mentioned it, you want to see my trait sheet, don't you? So curious! I like that about you.

Name: Riley
Trope: Manic Pixie Dream Boy (sub-type of Manic Pixie Dream Girl)
Age: 17
Birthday: June 6, Gemini
General physical description: Tall enough, but not lanky. Toned enough, but not a gym rat. Green eyes.

Dark hair. Thick eyebrows that look brooding, but a killer smile to balance out that impression. Basically, hot—but in a non-threatening way.

Clothing style: Mix of trendy and vintage. Cool with girls choosing his clothes. I'll even let them put eyeliner on me, though only for special occasions.

Hobbies: Writing silly love songs and picking out chords on the guitar. Memorizing French poetry. Darts.

Talents: Dance moves to pull out in montages to show how quirky and fun I am, the right witty banter for every occasion, the ability to spout off platitudes and sound achingly sincere, ninety percent free-throw average (but not aggressive enough to actually play full court basketball). I could go on, but I'm starting to sound like I'm bragging, so I won't.

Strongest positive personality traits: Flexible, kind, excellent listener.

Strongest negative personality traits: Can be flighty, indecisive, superficial.

Ambitions: Am I allowed to have these?

Life philosophy: I still haven't found what I'm looking for.

Favorite foods: Pie. Chicken wings but only if they are from free-range chickens, though I'm good at pretending. If I ask you if the chicken was free-range, I hope you say yes even if you don't actually know, so I can eat my chicken with a clear conscience. Coffee latte with soy or almond milk unless it costs extra in which case I will begrudgingly have regular milk or creamer.

Phobias: Clowns.

Do you feel like you know me better now? Does this make me more sympathetic? It's important to me that you like me. Because the more you like me, the more you'll care about what happens to me, and the more likely it is you'll continue to read my story. And I want you to continue because I don't exist otherwise.

CHAPTER 3

I wake up in the morning with a mix of excitement and dread. I get to meet Zelda, but then I'll have to excuse myself and go to therapy. And I can't tell her about therapy, because I don't want her to think I'm a huge screwup.

When I step outside, I take a deep breath.

"Oh, Riley!" Cathy, my Crazy Cat Lady neighbor, trills. "Can you help me? Sprite got herself stuck in the tree again."

"Sure thing." I wave to assure Cathy that I've got her cat emergency covered, and I climb the blossoming cherry tree that Sprite loves so much. If there were Manic Pixie cats, Sprite would be one. She's not the talking sort, but she's a quirky quicksilver, with extreme white fluff and a pink heart-shaped nose. I click my tongue to get her attention, but she refuses to directly acknowledge me, instead opting for a prance on a slim, wobbly branch. She loses her balance and falls, but luckily I catch her and bring her down to the relative safety of Cathy's arms.

Cathy pinches my cheek to show her gratitude. "A nice boy like you—when are you going to get yourself a girlfriend?"

"One of these days," I assure her, and Zelda pops up in my mind.

Sprite curls herself around Cathy's neck like a scarf and purrs. Cathy ties her ratty bathrobe tighter. "Don't wait too long. Unless you want to end up like me."

I shudder. I like Sprite, but Cathy has at least another basketful of felines lurking in her apartment that she hides to avoid extra pet rent. I can sometimes hear their plaintive chorus of mews late at night through the walls. Is it possible for a Manic Pixie to turn into a Crazy Cat Person Type? Are existential ennui and extreme loneliness the triggers? I hope I never find out.

I've been to the Ooh La Latte Café before. In fact, it's one my favorite places. Favorite because the baristas don't charge extra to substitute almond milk in my latte. Favorite because they dim the overhead lights to simulate twilight, and the décor is faux old-world French. And now a favorite because Zelda enjoys their teas.

Last night I pored over Zelda's character trait sheet and learned she's into sci-fi movies, collecting rare comic books, and cosplay. And at the pool hall she wields her cue like a professional hustler, leaving broken egos in her wake.

I enter the café. Zelda lounges on a blue velvet loveseat in the corner under a canopy of tiny lights strewn over the ceiling like stars. She sits with her chin tilted up and one eyebrow quirked. There's a hint of a smile on her lips, like she's having all these fascinating, hilarious thoughts, but she'd never deign to share them with the likes of you. Nevertheless, I approach her after procuring my latte.

"Hey, Z. Which tea's a-brewing today?"

Zelda snickers and stretches her long legs out under the round marble table in front of her. "Double O Cinnamon. Shaken, not stirred."

"Sounds like you have a license to chill."

"Tragic, Riley." Zelda peers up at me. She wears her chunky brown glasses and bulky sweater like armor. And the silver Ti-22 pin at her collar completes this impenetrable impression, as it seems she chose titanium for a reason. Her judgment stings like a rampaging prickle of porcupines, deflating me more than the prospect of going to therapy.

"You wound me, fair maiden."

"Oh, don't pout." She scoots over to let me sit next to her, close enough that even in the hazy light I can see the flecks of green in her brown eyes. Score!

"How's work?" I start off with an easy question while I raid the condiment chalice at the center of the table and stir a packet of sugar into my coffee.

She shrugs. "Oh, you know, the usual Early Days stuff. Showing up at three a.m. and knocking on his bedroom window. Making snow angels in the park under the moonlight. Destroying a unicorn topiary to show how rebellious I am."

God, how I wish she were doing all that stuff with me.

Does Zelda lie awake at night like I do, wishing she could go Off-Page and have adventures she dreams up herself instead of following the scripts she is handed every day?

"How about you?" she asks.

"My next project has been delayed. The Author suffers from writer's block."

"Do you actually believe in writer's block?" The way her question drips with disdain hints at her position on the issue, and my instinct is to agree with her, even though I don't have an informed opinion. It's risky to insult Authors, though, especially in a public place where anyone or any hidden device could be eavesdropping. I don't need any more black marks on my record.

"This Author must believe in it."

Zelda smirks. "That's exactly what Finn would have said."

"Yeah. He taught me well."

I'm not surprised to learn she knew Finn. He got around. As the original Manic Pixie Dream Boy, Finn trained me when I first arrived in TropeTown. We became poker buddies and best friends who told each other everything—or so I thought. But some fatal flaw forced him to board the Termination Train without saying goodbye to me, and I never even knew he was having problems. Why couldn't he confide in me? I beat myself up about that a lot.

"May he never go out of print." Zelda offers up the traditional TropeTown blessing for the terminated.

We sip our respective caffeinated beverages in respectful silence. Soft piano music plays over the café's speakers, and Zelda taps her foot on the swirl-patterned rug beneath our table in perfect rhythm. I take a deep, satisfying breath of air freshened with baking baguettes.

As I'm working up the courage to ask Zelda what she's doing later and if she wants to do it with me, a troop of Plucky Street Urchins enters the café and starts a song and dance number. Lead Urchin, a soulful little boy with tousled hair and grubby cheeks, presents me with a long-stemmed rose.

"Buy a flower for your lady, mister!" he implores.

Would Zelda find such a gesture romantic or not? She might consider it ironically charming and blush, or she might judge it sociologically abhorrent and lecture me.

Before I can decide, the Trendy Barista chases Lead Urchin out with a broom. With her attention focused on him, she doesn't notice when the Supporting Urchins stuff their pockets with almond croissants and mini-quiches from the display counter.

Once she's swept them all outside, she slams the glass door behind them and turns to us, her only paying customers, with an apologetic expression.

"Can't they stay on their own side of the tracks?" she grumbles. She trades her broom for a mop and a bucket and begins attacking the muddy footprints the Plucky Street Urchins left as souvenirs.

Zelda sighs. "I'd better go."

"But . . ." I blurt but stop myself. If there's one thing I've learned from working on romantic comedies, it's that timing is everything.

"What is it?" she asks, but she's not present in the moment anymore. She's already far away, probably thinking about whatever's next on her agenda.

I make up a quick cover. "You haven't savored your Double O Cinnamon to the last drop."

She slides her mug over until its rim touches the rim of my mug. Hers features the pink, glossy imprint of her lips. "Would you like a taste? It's all yours," she says in a flirty voice, and I nearly fall over.

"Uh, thank you," I say. "I would like that very much."

She gets up, does a little sexy spin so that her skirt swirls around her legs, and saunters out of the café without a backward glance. It takes me about five minutes before I can stand up without making a scene, if you know what I mean. By the time I remember to taste her tea, it's cold.

CHAPTER 4

I unfold the copy of Zelda's character trait sheet I've been carrying around in my pocket, hoping for additional insight into her psyche.

Name: Zelda
Trope: Manic Pixie Dream Girl (Sub-type: Geek Chic)
Age: 18
Birthday: December 6, Sagittarius
General physical description: Trim hourglass figure. High cheekbones. Hazel eyes. Dark hair. Basically, hot—but in a non-threatening way.
Clothing style: Chunky glasses, T-shirts with science- and comics-related graphics, cardigans, skirts, tights, clunky boots. Loves hair accessories and the color yellow.
Hobbies: Playing pool, badminton, and croquet. Reading graphic novels and classic literature. Birdwatching.
Talents: Rollerblading backwards. Sarcasm. Tying a cherry stem with tongue.
Strongest positive personality traits: Generous, honest, and adventurous.

Strongest negative personality traits: Can be harsh and careless. Inconsistent.

Ambitions: Live authentically.

Life philosophy: Make the most of every minute.

Favorite foods: Tea, egg salad and watercress sandwiches. Scones. Tropical fruit. Pizza.

Phobias: Globophobia (fear of balloons popping).

CHAPTER 5

My steps feel more solid once I leave the cobblestone of the Culinary District for the smooth black asphalt of the Administration District. The border is demarcated with a painted red-dotted line, like on a map, and fanatically maintained by Macho Construction Workers, who seal today's coat as I pass.

This part of town always smells sterile to me, as if it just recently emerged from factory-sealed packaging. Everything polished. Nothing out of place. Only the people give it any sort of personality.

Case in point: a group of Crotchety Old Men presently slows my progress toward the Healing Center. They weave and bob in front of me. If this were a Novel, I could be fashionably late, enter with a perfectly crafted one-liner, and everyone would laugh and forgive my tardiness as part of my charm. But here in TropeTown, I'd get a black mark in my permanent file, so I skirt the edge of the group and dash past, mumbling an apology.

"What's that, boy?" one of them yells, cupping a hand around one ear. "Where ya off to in such a rush? Gotta learn to respect your elders."

"Healing Center." I turn my head and project my voice. "Council-ordered group therapy."

The men gasp in horror and scramble away as fast as their walkers and canes will allow. One raises a gnarled fist. "Get off my lawn!"

My next obstacle is a posse of Cloyingly Cute Children who have chalked up the middle of the street with a giant hop-scotch maze. The No-Nonsense Street Cleaners are no doubt on their way to hose it down, but until then, I have to play to pass. A girl in pigtails hands me a bottle cap, and I use my best wind-up pitch to get it to land on the penultimate square. The children cheer me on as I skip and hop my way through their course.

After passing Town Hall, I finally make it to the Healing Center. It's the tallest building in West TropeTown, aka the Right Side of the Tracks, and its cream-colored outside walls gleam with the intention of making visitors feel safe and welcome.

I take a spin through the front revolving door three times just for the fun of it, emerging dizzy enough that the white and gray arrow pattern on the lobby floor seems to beckon me back to the bank of chrome elevators.

Behavioral Therapy is on the ninth floor, so I push the call button. The doors open, revealing a trifecta of animals engaged in a heated discussion. I wince, because I don't want to get my black jeans all fuzzed up and make a bad first impression, but I don't have time to wait for another elevator or I'll be tardy.

I know: #fictionalworldproblems.

I step in and position myself in the corner farthest from the Talking Beast brawl. My floor button is already lit.

"And to make it worse, they called me up and told me my picture will be on the cover," a brown and white collie in a blue windbreaker and sunglasses says.

A dashing red squirrel wearing a plaid bowtie chirps at him. "There you go again with the humblebrag. When has a Stock Squirrel ever made the cover? I wish I had your problems."

The collie sighs and cocks his head like he wants his chin scratched. "You know that means I die at the end. Again."

"Yeah," a raccoon in a trench coat pipes up. "But you'll get a noble death, and all the Developeds will cry over you and give you a funeral. My parts all end with me in a trash can facing down the barrel of a shotgun."

"In mine, I'm skinned and eaten for cheap protein." The squirrel jumps on the raccoon's shoulder, as if to show solidarity for the plight of non-domesticated animals in fiction. "Or I end up as roadkill."

I wait for the tiniest pause in their conversation to offer up some pseudo-philosophy unsolicited. "No matter how small they are in the grand scheme of things, everyone's own issues seem big to them."

"You don't look *wise* or *old* enough to be a Wise Old Mentor." The raccoon wriggles his whiskers in what seems like contempt. I could be reading into things, though. I tend to do that.

"Are you our replacement New Age Therapist?" The collie wags his tail, and tiny dog hairs are whisked in my direction.

"No." I shuffle my feet in an attempt to dodge his fur bullets. "I'm in therapy, like you. First meeting."

The squirrel blinks at me. "Sucks to be us. Well, at least the pie is good."

"The pie?" I ask. I freaking love pie.

"Pie is mandatory at every session," the squirrel explains. "The union made sure of that."

"Back on topic! You have the attention span of a squirrel!" the collie barks. "The human does have a point about comparative suffering. You shouldn't make me feel like my problems are unworthy of being addressed just because there are those who are worse off than I am."

"I can do whatever I want! It's called having agency. Look into it." The squirrel jumps down from the raccoon's back and makes a break for the doors as soon as the elevator dings.

The collie growls and chases after him. The raccoon shakes his head. "Eight weeks of group therapy with those two. I'd rather be trapped in an endless loop of trash dump loitering."

"At least there's pie," I tell him.

He waves his paw and saunters off. I brush my hand over my pants, but the fabric and fur have a fatal attraction.

When I step out of the elevator and into the wide hallway, a speck of silver catches my attention. I bend down to pluck it out from the thick pile of the taupe carpet. It's a round pin about a quarter of the size of my palm, and it has an "O" and an "8" printed on it—the periodic symbol for oxygen—so obviously my first thought is Zelda must have dropped it. But why would she be up on this floor?

I tuck the oxygen pin in my pants pocket and continue on.

CHAPTER 6

I arrive at Room 9393 at eight a.m. on the dot and mentally give myself a series of increasingly difficult high-five moves for my punctuality. When I open the door and saunter in, the smell of cinnamon and cherries hits hard, and my stomach rumbles. The room screams coziness, with walls painted the color of spring leaves and dotted with motivational posters featuring self-satisfied Tropes: *ALL THAT GLITTERS . . . IS A SUCCESSFUL GOLD DIGGER. THE GAMBLER . . . KNOWS WHEN TO HOLD 'EM.*

The group's New Age Therapist greets me with her roadside-billboard smile. Per her type, she wears a loose tank top, yoga pants, and a flowery scarf tied around her dreadlocks. A bracelet of wooden prayer beads hugs her right wrist. "Hey, everyone. Jazz hands for our latest addition to the group—Riley."

I glance around the room. The pie summons me from a side table. Two girls sit on folding chairs. I don't know them, but I've seen them around. It's a small world after all.

"You're a *boy!*" This obvious statement comes from a girl in a white dress and funky-patterned fuchsia tights. Her face registers surprise in the perfect imitation of a kewpie doll.

Based on her reaction and her messy blond hair and shockingly red lips, I figure she must be the Naïve sub-type of the MPDG Trope.

"Yeah, didn't you hear, Mandy?" a girl coming in behind me says. Her tone has an edge to it, like lemonade spiked with vodka. My whole body freezes with the certainty that this voice belongs to Zelda.

She swishes by me with her trademark smirk. Zelda is in therapy too. Zelda is in therapy *with me*.

It's both awesome and alarming. Because now she knows I'm messed up, and maybe she won't want to date me. But then, if she's here, she must also be kind of messed up, right? So who is she to judge?

Zelda continues. "They officially expanded the parameters of the Manic Pixie Dream Girl Trope a few seasons ago to include the incredibly groundbreaking concept of a boy in a story who exists solely to contribute to the emotional epiphany of a Developed."

"Oooh, that's so progressive and daring of some Authors." Mandy giggles. "To put a boy through all this Manic Pixie nonsense? No offense, Riley."

"None taken." I find a seat. Zelda sits opposite to me in the circle. When she catches my eye, she acknowledges me with a saucy wink. Ooooh. Maybe she's into screw-ups? Maybe I do have a chance!

"So, thanks for that illuminating definition, Zelda," the New Age Therapist says. When I squint, I can make out *Angela* on her nametag. I would have expected something less mundane, like Moonbeam.

"Happy to help," Zelda says.

Angela places a folder in my lap. "We're still waiting on

Nebraska, but that might take a while, so let's go ahead and get started. For the benefit of our newcomer, I am going to go over our goals for therapy."

I open the folder to the first page and follow along as Angela reads word for word from it.

1. Embrace your Trope and accept that deviations from expected behavior cannot be tolerated
2. Acknowledge that the Author is always right in matters including but not limited to plot, dialogue, and character motivations.
3. Gain an understanding of your personal shortcomings that have led to your infractions and develop strategies for dealing with them before they destroy you.

"As for the rules, Riley, you can go over them yourself and speak to me privately later if you have any concerns, okay?"

I nod as I flip through the folder. There are so many pages. I am pretty sure I will never actually read them.

Angela turns her attention back to the girls. "Chloe, you're up today. Tell us why you're here."

"Hey everybody. I'm Chloe." She brushes her chunky bangs back from her big blue eyes.

Clearly the Freaky Chic sub-type of the MPDG Trope, Chloe's gorgeous, with porcelain skin and dark hair. But because she's supposed to be approachable, she probably always makes faces or tells dirty jokes or trips over her own feet.

"I'm here because my last Author said I was too unreliable. Like, come on, she ordered a Manic Pixie. What did she expect? What a newbie."

Zelda stiffens. "Are you sure you should be saying that? Authors may be listening in on us."

"We inhabit a safe space here," Angela insists. "It's perfectly fine to voice any and all feelings. Let's work on bringing ourselves down a path to healing and whole-heartedness."

"That Author *is* a total newbie," I blurt out. Something about Chloe makes me want to throw coats over puddles of root beer in the cantina for her so she never has to get her feet sticky. I'm sure she's quite used to that.

Everyone, minus Angela, chimes in until it becomes a mantra. "Newbie Author! Newbie Author!"

Chloe gets up and moves her arms and legs around like she's a robot learning how to dance. It's almost painful to see her lithe body contorting in such inelegant fits.

"Go Chloe, go Chloe, go, go, go Chloe!" The rest of us get up and imitate her movements as best we can while we laugh at full throttle. It's surprisingly difficult to dance so badly. I've never been so immediately comfortable in a group setting before. These girls are clearly my kindred spirits.

Chloe catches her foot on the tassels of the rug and falls backward into her chair with a dull bang. We immediately sober and sit again.

"That's my signature move," Chloe explains. "You know how in a lot of teen movies there's a dance scene at some point?"

"Oh yeah," Zelda says. "And if your character is lucky enough to live until the end, it's usually the big climatic set piece."

"Right." Chloe clears her throat. "At the big dance-off, my Authors always make me do that dance. And the Developeds come away feeling less insecure about themselves because I made a fool of myself."

"And you don't like that?" Angela asks.

Chloe shimmies. "Actually, that dance is really fun. I love it. But what I object to is being forced to do it in a setting where the Author is trying to impart a life lesson about self-esteem."

"We don't ever get to do anything purely for our own satisfaction," I say. "Or to further our own goals. Everything we do is in service of a plot that centers on someone else. And . . . that sucks." It's the first time I've acknowledged this out loud, so I'm a bit nervous about the group's reaction.

Zelda claps, slowly. "Hear, hear." Her validation is both calming and thrilling.

Angela pushes her hands forward as if to hold back our objections. "But isn't that our purpose? As Tropes, we are made to serve the stories we are written into. We must learn to accept the things we cannot change. Because if we don't do our jobs, then we're at risk for termination."

Mandy visibly blanches. "So you're saying if we can't accept the role someone else puts us in, we're basically asking to be terminated?"

Angela raises her eyebrows, and an uncomfortable silence descends. Of course, I think of Finn, since he's the only person close to me who has ever been terminated. Did burnout have something do with his fate? Did he get so tired of his Manic Pixie role that he simply gave up and let himself be led away to the Termination Train? I have trouble imagining it.

"Maybe this isn't all there is," Zelda says. She rubs a ring on her left pinkie. "Maybe there's more out there, and the Council just . . ."

Angela sharply cuts her off. "Let's get back on track, shall we?" she says. Despite her earlier claim that therapy is a safe space, she seems alarmed that the conversation has taken this turn. Maybe the Council really is surveilling us. "Chloe was telling us why she's here."

Zelda removes her pinkie ring and slips it into a pocket in her jacket.

Chloe purses her lips and brushes at her bangs, which are back in her eyes. "Yeah, so anyway, in my last part, the Author was staging this dance scene, and I knew she was going to force me to do my signature Awkward Robot. But, like, I wasn't feeling it. The Central Developed was this super-hot football player, and all the clues up until then pointed at him secretly being in love with the Shy Girl Next Door."

Zelda smirks. "Shy Girls Next Door can't dance their way out of an environmentally friendly paper bag."

"Exactly," Chloe continues. "So here was my chance to impress the Central Developed and blow away my competition. I took it, and that pissed off my Author. She ordered a Revision."

"What is so unusual about that?" Angela asks. She readjusts her headscarf, as if she's afraid it might run off if she doesn't tie it down properly. "Revisions are industry standard after all."

"Well, I refused to show up. The Author lodged a complaint and killed me off in summary narration."

"That's the worst!" Mandy says sympathetically.

"Now I've been branded as unreliable and no one wants to work with me." Chloe pulls a thin gold chain from under her geometric-print peasant blouse and rubs a finger along her collarbone. "Therapy is supposed to help me refocus. I need to accept my place in the narrative hierarchy and do as I'm told."

Angela struts over to a particularly garish motivational poster and presents it like it belongs in the Sistine Chapel or something. "Embrace your Trope," she reads. "It's who you are!"

While it's true each of us in this room was created with the express purpose of fulfilling the guidelines of our Trope, obviously there is something faulty in our profiles or we wouldn't be here, in therapy, facing termination.

"Remember," Angela says. "The Author is always right."

We're all quiet enough that Angela must think she's browbeaten us into total submission. She returns to her seat, satisfied. "Very good, Chloe. So what are you going to work on going forward?"

"The Author is always right," Chloe says in a grudging tone.

"Do you agree with that, Riley?" Angela asks.

"Yes, ma'am," I say, but when she turns her head, I wink at Zelda. She winks back and just like that, we're engaged in a veritable wink-fest. It's revoltingly adorable, and I'm seized by a powerful urge to catch her after the meeting and ask her out.

"Excellent!" Angela claps her hands together. "Since it's your first day, why don't you do us the honor of partitioning the pie?"

"I thought you'd never ask!" I practically teleport to the pie table and cut a serving for each of us, artfully arranging each piece on purple paper plates. But when I turn to hand Zelda the first portion, my eager smile droops.

Zelda has already left.

CHAPTER 7

After wolfing down our pie, Mandy and Chloe invite me to hang out with them at the cantina. I agree, and soon I'm drowning my disappointment over Zelda's disappearing act in a delicious root beer float. Mandy and Chloe act like we're life-long pals, and it surprises me how effortless it feels to hang out with them. I'm not at all worried about impressing them, like I am with Zelda. I can be myself. I haven't had this sort of companionship since Finn disappeared. I've missed it.

The Administration District's sole cheap eating establishment, the cantina fills a large and drafty space reminiscent of an aircraft hangar. Maybe it used to be one, though we don't need airplanes in TropeTown. Food stations line all four walls and white, round Formica tables dot the rest of the room.

The drinks station queue moves quickly. I grab a tray, fill up three chilled mugs with root beer, add in a scoop of ice cream to each, and pay for it all by selecting my items on the screen and inserting my chip card into the reader. Neither Mandy nor Chloe objects to my grand act of chivalry. Chloe even thanks me.

The cantina echoes with conversation and clinking cutlery. At this time of day, free seats are scarce. Mandy tap dances in front of a Mysterious Loner Dude who takes up a whole table. He's been writing brooding poems in a leather-bound journal with a fountain pen, but her manic energy drives him to pick up his inkpot and slink away, leaving the table to us.

Once we spread out, I distribute our floats. Mandy digs in her purse and pulls out some pink bendy straws in the shape of hearts. "Do everything you do with passion!" she exclaims.

I impale the ice cream foam with the straw. "Did you learn that in therapy?"

"Hmmm . . ." She squeezes her earlobe. "No. I think I came preprogrammed with positive, life-affirming aphorisms. Didn't you?"

"*I* did." Chloe burps out a full sentence: "Don't just do it, do it better!" She giggles. Obviously she's so cute, she has internalized that she can get away with such questionable manners.

"I never really thought about it," I admit. But now that I do think about it, I realize I couldn't tell you how or when I learned certain facts—I just seem to know them. In fact, I make obscure references to philosophy or geography as a party trick. "What's the capital of Mali?"

Chloe raises her hand, as if to answer a question in class. "Um, Riley. Non sequitur."

I pretend that's really her answer. "Nope."

"Fine." She lets out an exaggerated sigh. "Timbuktu."

"Actually, it's Bamako."

"Timbuktu is the ancient scholarly capital of the trans-Saharan route, though," Chloe says. "And a UNESCO World Heritage Site. Doesn't that count for something?"

I laugh. "You're such a nerd. I love it." Again, I'm gob-smacked by how well we all click. Maybe it's by design? Are Manic Pixies just meant to get along with one another because we're so fun loving and chill at heart? But then, why do I feel mere camaraderie with Mandy and Chloe, whereas I'm crushing on Zelda?

Chloe sticks her tongue out at me. "Well, I've always wanted to go. The photos I've seen are gorgeous."

We nurse our root beer floats in silence for a moment. No need to ask why she hasn't gone. We all know there's not much call for the Manic Pixie Trope in books set in that region of the world.

"Nebraska never showed up today," Mandy says.

"Shocking," Chloe says dryly.

Mandy finishes off her float, leaving red lipstick stains all over her pink bendy straw. "Do you think we should check up on her?"

"Looking for Nebraska is a waste of time," Chloe declares. "You won't find her until she wants to be found."

"Do you know Nebraska?" Mandy asks me.

"I don't think so." Perhaps one of the biggest misconceptions about Manic Pixies is that we are these super social creatures with giant extrovert personalities. We're actually introverts at heart, and we tend to latch on to one or two people. I spent most of my free time hanging out one-on-one with Finn, up until he boarded the Termination Train.

"Don't feel bad," Chloe says. "Nebraska overbooks herself so that she never has time for anything but work and sleep and the occasional therapy session. And that's the way she likes it. She's been in TropeTown for decades, longer than any other Manic Pixie. She's Legacy."

"Whoa!" I say. "That's swanky." Legacy Tropes live in TropeTown Heights, a gated community with mansions and limos and a yellow-brick road. They get all sorts of other perks, too—for instance, unlike the rest of us, Legacies get to pick and choose which projects they take on. Why is she in therapy when she has it so good?

"It is," Mandy confirms. "Nebraska invited me over once. She has the most amazing blue diamond chandelier."

Chloe sighs. "My blue ceramic lamp can't compete with that. And if an Author doesn't hire me soon, I'll be evicted and end up on the Wrong Side of the Tracks. Then I'll be smashing cockroaches with a blue plastic flashlight."

Mandy pats Chloe on the head. "I know what will cheer you up! Fortune cookie roulette!" She pulls out a few handfuls of wrapped fortune cookies from her bag and arranges them in a peace sign in front of Chloe.

Chloe grabs one from the center and cracks it open. "Prepare yourself for a new adventure," she reads aloud.

"See?" Mandy claps her hands together in delight. "A new job is definitely on its way."

"Moving to a hovel could also count as a new adventure," Chloe points out, her shoulders slumping.

"But you'd train those pesky cockroaches and sell them to a circus in no time," I joke.

Chloe smiles. "Thanks, Riley. You're a good guy." She pushes one of the cookies in my direction. "Your turn."

I open it and read: "Love is close, but only claimed through courage." Even my fortune thinks I should ask Zelda out. Maybe Crazy Cat Lady Cathy has a side job writing fortunes.

"Ooooh. Who's the lucky girl, Riley?" Mandy extracts a tiny ukulele from her bag and starts strumming the traditional wedding song. "Maybe someone in our therapy circle?"

"Stop that," Chloe chastises. "Manic Pixies are not meant to fall for each other."

"I just think star-crossed lovers are so romantic!"

My heart struggles to beat, sensing a crushing blow. "Why star-crossed?"

Chloe taps the therapy rules folder in my lap. "Gotta read the rules, Riley. It's a termination-worthy transgression to date anyone while you're both active in the group."

CHAPTER 8

Before I can wallow in self-pity, the glow of an Author summoning lights me up. This is it.

Showtime.

I excuse myself from the table and let my finger hover over the 'go' button on my official TropeTown employee band. Starting a new job is a little like jumping off a cliff with a blindfold on, but this is my purpose—my reason for being—and I don't have a choice anyway. When I press the button, I'm swept into the backstage area of a Work-In-Progress.

My body spends the requisite 33.3 seconds adjusting to its new plane of existence. This stage of the travel process dulls all the senses. When you snap out of it, the most noticeable side effect is extreme thirst.

I make a beeline for the craft services table. I snag a green smoothie from a tray and gulp it down greedily.

You can always tell the production budget from the quality of the food, and judging by the delectable spread, I'd say this novel sold in a major deal. Which would be pretty risky on the publisher's part, considering the project is obviously not finished. Must be high concept and on trend.

Other than the food, though, the backstage area is

unremarkable and indistinguishable from any of the other projects I've worked on. Green paint is chipping off the walls, sawdust drifts on the floor, and cobwebs creep in the corners. A couple of empty clothes racks for wardrobe changes stand idle. Next to the stage door is a line of green chairs, each supporting stacks of paper of varying heights. Before I can investigate further, a girl approaches me.

She checks me out thoroughly, like five whole seconds from head to toe, and I return the favor because it's only fair. She's pretty, but from her sleek ponytail and practical shoes, I can tell she's no-frills. Probably an uptight, studious sort that needs to learn how to let loose. Which is likely why the Author ordered my Trope.

"I'm Ava," she says finally. "The Central Developed."

Being welcomed by the Central Developed is a good indicator that I play a crucial role in her story. But odds are she won't play a crucial role in *my* story. When I'm done, I'll leave an Understudy copy of myself to perform my duties. While Ava toils here reliving this novel ad infinitum for her Readers, I'll be off to other parts. Unless I plant.

You plant when you decide to stay inside the novel you've been working on, instead of letting a copy take over. Planting is like marriage without the possibility of divorce, because once you plant, that's it—no other stories or characters to explore.

Ever.

Traditionally far too flighty to settle down, Manic Pixies rarely plant. But Finn always said if a Manic Pixie ever hit the jackpot of a genuinely happy ending, such a permanent move might be tempting.

I can't imagine ever choosing to put down roots with Ava though, at least not based on my first impression.

After a pause long enough to piss her off, I introduce myself. "Hi Ava. I'm Riley."

"I don't need your TropeTown name." She looks at her fingernails instead of at me. "Around here you're called Marsden."

Marsden? Is this Author smoking cloves? I console myself by glancing back at the craft table and counting three pies.

"So what's the synopsis?"

Ava huffs. "Who knows? The Author hasn't even provided an outline, which is incredibly frustrating to a type-A control freak like me."

"Well, I'd think we'd be past the inciting incident already, right?" The inciting incident is the departure from the Central Developed's regular routine that starts the action. In Ava's case, I'd guess her perfect Student Council President Boyfriend broke up with her. Or maybe she got a B on her report card, putting the Ivy League out of her reach.

(Oh, and if you're wracking your brain trying to figure out the inciting incident in *my* story, it was the letter from the TropeTown Council, which is the reason I'm now in therapy. And being in therapy is the reason I can't date Zelda, at least not while we're both in the group. And not being able to date Zelda is the reason I'm sad, but I can't think about that now, because I have a job to do.)

"You'd think that, but you'd be wrong." Ava throws up her hands and stalks over to the green chair with her name on it. She shows me all her blank pages. "She's writing scenes out of order."

It's always something with these Authors. Why can't they just sit their butts down, do the nine-to-five grind like everyone else, and write in a linear fashion? Is that so freaking hard?

"Have you seen her yet?" I ask. Central Developeds actually

score face time with the Author Off-Page, so the Author can figure out how they tick. Authors never meet with Tropes because they figure they already know us inside out.

"Yes. We did Pilates together, and she cranked up her book playlist. She said she spent weeks coming up with songs that exude the atmosphere of the piece." Ava snorts. "It felt kind of like a waste of time, honestly."

"Hmmm." I try to sound agreeable even though I don't agree. I would love the chance to hang out with someone from Reader World, and she's taking it for granted. "What kind of music was it?"

"Loud and weird." She puts her hands on her hips. "You ask a lot of questions for a Trope."

It takes all of my willpower to bite down a retort. I've dealt with Developed privilege like this before. Central Developeds can be pretty ignorant when it comes to Tropes—regarding us as lesser, equating us with robots. I'd love to set her straight, but I can't risk alienating myself on the first day and getting another complaint letter on my record. So I take a deep breath and force a smile. "Just want this project to go as smoothly as possible. I'm sure I'll enjoy working with you."

My genial attitude seems to mollify her. The green light blinks on over the stage door, signaling the Author's readiness.

I follow Ava onto the bare set, which resembles a giant soundstage with a green screen for special effects. The setting manifests as the Author writes it. Even though I'll never see her, I experience the full force of her clacking laptop keys. As she types, asphalt with evenly spaced yellow lines appears under our feet. The light changes to simulate a cloudy, overcast day. In the background, a nondescript building takes shape, and a sign declares its function as the DMV.

Many of the details of this parking lot setting remain vague, not only because this is a first draft, but also because most Readers can visualize this place without the Author having to provide excessive description that will slow down the story. To us, the characters, it can be a bit unnerving, because often we only physically see a few important scene markers, and the rest is kind of a messy blur we have to fill in with our own imaginations.

If the Author describes our wardrobe, we pause to go find our pieces waiting on the racks offstage and change into them. But today she doesn't.

She continues to type furiously, setting up Marsden as the new boy in town. Marsden and Ava have their meet-cute while they wait for their respective rides. They've both just passed their driving tests, and they discuss the fact that Ava got a perfect score while Marsden nearly failed.

Marsden senses something is bothering Ava, and he's determined to lift her spirits, which he does by choreographing a Driver's Test Dance on the spot, but then Ava's best friend, the snobby Samantha, arrives to pick Ava up and makes fun of Marsden, even though he's, like, so hot for a high school guy and all.

Good times.

It's a tough day of rough drafting. I swear I develop whiplash from all the head nodding and bounding about I'm forced to do. By the time Ava flounces off to a side door marked "Private" and I'm beamed home, I'm so grateful for my pillow that I weep tears of exhaustion into it before passing out.

CHAPTER 9

The next day, two additional girls show up in group therapy. Angela doesn't introduce them, so I assume they're regulars who probably had to work yesterday. The only valid excuses for missing a meeting are work and illness, and these rosy-cheeked babes are portraits of health.

Sadly, Zelda acts like she doesn't register me at all. She keeps clenching her fists like she wants to punch someone. I'm dying to get her alone and find out how much longer she has to attend this group. How much longer I'll have to wait until I'm allowed to ask her out. Waiting is the worst.

"Attention ladies and Riley," Angela says. "Today we're going to start out with a super uplifting exercise. Close your eyes, please."

Groans abound, but I close mine. With my vision out of commission, my sense of smell sharpens and alerts me to the scent of apples and nutmeg. My mouth waters. Why can't we *start* with eating pie?

"Raise your hand if you've ever felt alone," Angela instructs.

I raise my hand. Of course.

"Now. Open your eyes."

Everyone has raised a hand. Chloe has even raised both. We sheepishly put them down.

"See? Isn't it reassuring to know you're not alone in feeling alone? Just think about that when you've got the loneliness blues."

It's typical inspirational mumbo jumbo, but it's surprisingly effective. Naturally, I'd feel even less alone if I were dating Zelda. I keep sneaking glances at her, but her gaze is locked on the floor. Lucky floor.

"You're never lonely if you love your own company." Another girl bursts into our circle and plops an enormous handbag down next to the last empty chair—the one beside Angela. She stretches languidly, not seeming to care she's late. Of all of us, she's the most uniquely put together. She wears her hair jagged, the tips red as if dipped in blood. Her collarbones jut out, sharp as blades. If she has any soft parts, she keeps them well hidden under her giant sweater and clashing leggings. Whoever she is, she's the epitome of the Beautiful Mess subtype of the MPDG Trope.

"Nice of you to show up, Nebraska." Angela's usually silky voice cracks a bit.

"You know I live for therapy." Nebraska takes a bow and arranges herself neatly in her chair.

So this is TropeTown's only MPDG Legacy. I'm not surprised she looks like a teenager, even though she's been around so long. Tropes can resemble vampires in that way. I'm on the opposite end of the spectrum, though my simulated memories allow me to function as a teenager despite my lack of years.

"Do you want to share, today?" Angela asks her.

"Okay. Here's what bothers me." Nebraska twirls a finger absentmindedly in one of the longer strands of her hair. "Like,

I'm offered a part, right?" She says *offered* because as a Legacy, she reserves the right to turn down jobs. "And I get my hopes up because I'm the title character. I think, okay! Finally. I'm going to be allowed to really explore myself within this role. Growth! Maybe I'll even have my own happy ending. And at the beginning it looks promising. I have my own interests and hobbies. The Author writes all these juicy scenes for me where I pursue relationships that have nothing to do with the Central Developed. I state my goals and even hint at my own personal desire line. I wake up in the morning excited to go to work."

I find myself nodding along to all of this, even though I'm new, have only played a couple parts so far, and have never achieved title character status.

Nebraska pauses dramatically, folding her arms around herself and striking a wounded pose that seems calculated to elicit the maximum amount of sympathy.

"But then it all goes to hell in a high-fashion handbag," Zelda says, perhaps pondering some tough disappointments of her own.

"It always does," Nebraska agrees. "In my latest novel, I fool around with the Central Developed and then kill myself. And he's, like, beside himself, trying to figure out what he did wrong and searching for answers. It's so unfair for my character to get shafted like that."

"You shouldn't take it personally," Angela says. "These are characters you play. They aren't you."

"I know what Nebraska means." I didn't mean it to come out as forcibly as it does, but apparently this is a topic I'm passionate about, so I run with it. "Even if they are only parts, every part we take on informs our own sense of self. And when we're forced to live the same quirks over and over, those quirks start to define us. I mean, look at us—we're all typecast. I don't even know most of you, and I can already guess your sub-types."

Zelda claps. "Ooh. A challenge!"

All eyes are on me. I'm hit with a wave of paralyzing fear, and my inner introvert scolds my outer extrovert for always recklessly seeking the spotlight. I simultaneously want to crawl under my chair and jump on top of it.

"Do mine!" One of the girls who wasn't here yesterday leans forward. She has out-of-control blond curls and a vintage leather jacket. Her eyes sparkle with mischief behind her round, rose-colored glasses, and she has a giant set of headphones around her swan-like neck.

I gulp. Okay. I'm doing this. "I bet you have a band T-shirt under that jacket."

She laughs, and I'm reminded of wind chimes. "Right you are." She opens her jacket to reveal an oversized black tee with a faded and peeling graphic of the Allman Brothers. "I'm Lucy, by the way. But my friends call me Sky. Like, Lucy in the Sky with Diamonds."

"Okay, Sky. May I call you Sky?"

Sky nods.

"I diagnose you with a severe case of the Wild Child variant of MPDG," I intone in my most officious-sounding voice.

"Right you are!" She rewards me with her wind-chime laugh. I find myself plotting ways to hear that laugh. "And it means I go to rock concerts constantly, which I love."

Zelda claps, again. Is she subtly mocking me? "Sky is too easy. Try George." She taps the leg of the girl next to her, the other girl who wasn't here yesterday. "She's a tough one."

A smile lights up George's perfect heart-shaped face. She sports *Little House on the Prairie* braids and clean-scrubbed skin. There's a motorcycle helmet under her chair, even though no one in TropeTown owns motor vehicles. She squirms in her seat and constantly pulls at the sleeves of her crushed velvet hoodie with fingers stained by purple ink.

I take a chance. "Hmmm . . . I'm going to say . . . Bubbly Badass."

George extends her bare feet and wiggles her painted black toenails. "Did the skulls give me away?"

Nebraska yawns. I can already tell she has a habit of checking out when the attention is not focused on her. "Georgina has been here the *second* longest of us all. She's hired for a bunch of gigs because she's so fresh and fun." Though her words seem complimentary, her tone is biting.

"Don't call me Georgina."

Nebraska dismisses George with a backward twist of her wrist, causing an armful of metal bangles to clink together.

The room buzzes and a warm, yellow light forms around Zelda. She perks up considerably, even granting me a much-sought-after wink before she presses her bracelet button. She fades out as she's beamed over to her current novel of employment and my spirits sink. I won't get the chance to talk to her today, either.

Angela sniffs. "Well, that's all very astute of you, Riley, but today we are hearing from Nebraska. Let's let her continue, shall we?"

Her reprimand is as subtle as a slap. I take a vow of silence until I can slice into the pie. With Zelda gone, only pie can salvage this session.

Nebraska's violet eyes bore into me. "Riley, is it?"

"Yeah." Vow of silence broken after 2.2 seconds. A new record!

"Finn spoke highly of you in his letters." She sashays over to me and extends her elegant hand. "Friends of Finn are friends of mine."

I shake her hand, stunned. Letters? Finn wrote Nebraska letters? File that under *More secrets Finn kept.*

"You can return to your seat now," Angela says, her cheerful veneer chipping at the edges. "And apparently I need to go over the rules of group therapy for the forgetful among us."

Nebraska looks from Angela to her bracelet. She flips Angela her ring finger and pushes the rarely-used lever that allows Tropes to visit their workplace without being summoned. The room buzzes again, and the familiar light forms around her. Instantly, she's gone. Apparently Nebraska would rather go off to hang around her unsatisfying job than accept Angela's authority.

Angela stomps over to the pie and stabs it with a fork. "Pie is served."

None of us move. Angela forces a smile. "You're all welcome to go whenever you want."

Even so, we wait until she leaves before we serve ourselves slices of pie.

I take a bite and gag. It tastes like turnips.

CHAPTER 10

Let's talk about expectations for a minute. You expect a pie, especially one smelling of apples and nutmeg, to delight your tongue with its tart sweetness. All you want is for that apple pie to fulfill its duty as an apple pie. You do not want to put that apple pie in your mouth and taste turnips, even if you're a fan of turnips.

It's the same principle with Tropes. Tropes continue to exist because they're expected, and people derive satisfaction from a certain amount of fulfilled expectation. (Even Manic Pixies are predictable in their unpredictability.) Obviously, that amount varies, which is why some Readers gravitate toward Trope-heavy tomes and others seek out experimental fiction. But we Tropes get hired for the avant-garde stuff, too, because even the most adventurous of Readers needs something familiar to latch onto every once in a while.

Authors come to us to fill out their fictional landscapes, because not every situation or character needs to be Developed. Some of them just need to be apple pies that taste like apple pie.

CHAPTER 11

"Can anyone help me move a giant pane of glass out of my apartment?" Mandy asks us after dumping the disappointing apple pie in the trash.

The remaining girls all come up with excuses. Chloe needs to go to the employment office. Sky is off to knit fingerless gloves for her favorite Washed-Up Rock Stars. George mumbles something about a stripper pole and a sloth, and no one really wants to ask more questions about that.

I agree, because I've got nothing better to do, and because with those doe eyes, Mandy could get a guy to do just about anything for her, even a guy who is gaga for another girl.

As we walk to Mandy's place, she chatters on and on about Chloe's joblessness, Sky's obsession with music, and George's quirky array of hobbies. She makes sure not to step on any cracks in the pavement. Nothing out of the ordinary for a Manic Pixie profile.

Mandy's apartment is located in the same sprawling complex as mine and features the same floor plan and standard-issue furniture. But that's where the similarities end, because glass takes up every free inch of space. Glass chickens. Glass cucumbers. Glass cupcakes, for fox sake.

Obviously I have to ask. "What's up with the massive quantities of glass?"

"That's all Clark. My ex, as of last night. He's a Sensitive Nice Guy who spends too much time at the glass factory."

"So what sins did he commit to become your ex?"

Mandy rolls her eyes. "OMG . . . maybe shower me with useless glass knick-knacks?"

I pick up a flat, brown, smooth piece of glass resembling an ear.

"I'm pretty sure that's meant to be a spleen," she says.

"Well, Mandy, spleens are actually quite useful organs. They help us fight off infections."

She mimics my know-it-all tone exactly. "Well, Riley, *glass* spleens are actually quite useless. Especially when given as a part of an ill-advised Grand Romantic Gesture after a big fight."

"Good point."

Mandy extracts two pairs of work gloves from a drawer and throws a pair at me. "Catch."

She has excellent aim. And she may look fragile, but when we heft the pane of glass between us, she carries her share of the weight.

"Where are we going with this?" I ask as we maneuver the cumbersome pane through her door.

"See, this pane of glass represents my relationship with Clark," Mandy explains. "If we can carry it all the way to the factory without it breaking, then I'll give Clark another chance."

"Carrying a large pane of glass through town is tempting fate in a big way."

She grins and smacks an imprint of her red lips on the glass. "Exactly."

Well, you can guess what happens next, I'm sure, because this situation has played out so many times, it's become a Trope. Someone's riding a bicycle or driving a car and the inevitable crash goes down. You expect it. And when that glass does break into a trillion tiny shards, you're proud of yourself because you saw it coming.

In this case, it's a clown car that does the deed. And it's my clown phobia that forces me to flee the scene. Mandy skips after me, giggling.

"That was fun." She spins and screams out, "Hey Clark! I'm done with you. And with your glass chicken, too!"

When we get back to Mandy's, she makes space on her linoleum entry floor and rolls out a plastic tarp. She arms me with a hammer and tells me to let loose.

"Are you sure?" I heft the heavy tool and take a tentative swing.

"Smash first, ask later." She sets the chicken sculpture on the tarp and pounds away until a mound of yellow shards feathers the tarp. She carefully picks up the broken pieces and glues them to her wall in a circular pattern with outward spokes, like a child's version of the sun.

I reach for the spleen, but she places a gloved-hand on my arm to stop me. "This must stay whole. It symbolizes my need to concentrate on healing right now rather than be pulled into more foolish escapades by my errant heart."

We spend the afternoon gleefully shattering glass and affixing it around the spleen, the centerpiece of her mosaic masterpiece.

Her art inspires me to ask if I can take some of the red glass home. I want to paste a heart on my wall as a reminder to take more chances.

She fills up a plastic bucket with the remains of a pair of giant lobster figurines for me and collapses on her couch. "See you tomorrow in therapy."

I blow her two friendly kisses in farewell. She catches them and pats them onto her cheeks.

Mandy's front door faces the complex's inner courtyard, a wide space that features tennis courts, a swimming pool, a playground with a jungle gym, and even a netted baseball diamond. When I walk out with my bucket, I'm distracted for a moment by a lively Little League game. Harried Helicopter Parents shout insults at the Stoic Umpire while an Unconventional Coach gives a Defining Moment Pep Talk to the Spunky Underdogs in the dugout. I don't need to stay to know how this one will turn out. Same story, different day.

CHAPTER 12

Back in my apartment, I throw myself passionately into my heart mosaic. I choose a spot opposite the sofa, so it can confront me when I wake in the morning and before I fall asleep at night. I spend an hour pasting the red shards into a fairly accurate depiction of an emoji heart (not an actual heart, though I'd excuse you for thinking that since Mandy has an actual spleen on her wall).

As I admire my handiwork, I hear scratching at my door.

When I open up, Sprite is sitting on my welcome mat. She rubs up against my legs and meows. She sniffs at my door frame with interest.

"You want to come in?" Normally, I wouldn't offer, but I haven't had visitors in a long time.

Sprite blinks like maybe she understands, but I know she can't because she's an Add-On—an accessory for Cathy, without the same level of agency those animals I saw in the Healing Center elevator have. She scampers into my entryway.

Maybe Sprite has transferred a little of bit of Cathy's zaniness to me, because I start to pretend Sprite is Zelda visiting me in cat form. To complete the illusion, I fumble in my pants pocket for the silver oxygen pin I found outside the Healing

Center elevator the day before yesterday and attach it to Sprite's silver collar. (Yes, I've worn the same pants three days in a row, and I'll probably wear them again tomorrow. I *am* a guy.)

Sprite saunters into my living room as if she owns the place. She is at least familiar with the layout and the furniture since Cathy's unit is identical. All of the units in this complex are standard-issue singles, with the exception of the family units, which are twice as large. Beyond the basics, we can personalize by visiting the Shopping District, but I have to admit I can't be bothered to spend much of my free time bargain hunting and dodging Mopey Mallrats. Also, collecting experiences trumps having a bunch of trinkets. Regardless, Sprite has to check everything out. She stands on her hind paws to get a better peek at the bookshelf.

"I bought comics to have more in common with you." I speak to Sprite as if she were Zelda, though I'd probably never be this honest with the actual Zelda. I set my bucket of glass on the top shelf so Sprite can't get into it and cut herself.

My sleeve catches on the dartboard next to the bookshelf. It reminds me of my marathon games with Finn. He used to come over all the time, and the place seems empty without his constant stream of puns. He claimed to have a disease called *Witzelsucht*, which is German for "addiction to wisecracking." The Germans truly do have a word for everything.

Sprite flicks her tail and meanders around the rest of the room, inspecting the two gray fabric wingback chairs and the matching sofa before jumping on the glass top of the coffee table where she leaves a little trail of kitty prints. Good thing housekeeping comes tomorrow. I don't mind a little disorder, as long as I can find everything, but dirt and grime make me twitchy.

She touches her pink nose against the globe standing on the table, right at the equator in the middle of the Pacific Ocean. "What are those black dots, you ask? Those are all the places I've worked." There are not many dots, as of yet, and I haven't actually been to those cities and towns, only the facsimiles Authors describe. Most of them fall in the United States, though one dot covers Amsterdam and one covers Cape Town, South Africa.

My guitar leans against the wall, and Sprite rubs up against the strings, producing a hollow sound. For the real Zelda, I might pick up the guitar and play the three chords every dabbler learns to woo women: G, C, and D. I'd make up a sweet yet witty song and Zelda would melt into my waiting arms. Sprite, however, hisses at the guitar, so no song for her!

Next Sprite visits my kitchen, which I splashed with blue paint one day when I felt restless. Finn used to say it looked like mermaids had swum across my granite countertops. Sprite meows in front of my fridge and licks her chops.

"What a neglectful host I am! I forgot to offer you a drink. I'm afraid I'm out of the Double O Cinnamon you hold in such high esteem." My standing grocery order will come tomorrow, too, though tea is never on my list, because tea is, well, not my cup of tea. I pour her a tiny saucer of almond milk, which she laps up daintily.

After she has her fill, we continue the tour. She scratches the rug in my bathroom and slides around in the tub. I have a vision of Zelda in her place, soaking in a frothy bubble bath, and if I stay any longer in this fantasy, I'm going to need a cold shower. "Let's move on, shall we?"

Of course, the next place Sprite wants to visit is my bedroom, and when I open the door, she heads straight for my perfectly made bed (pristine, in fact, because I always sleep on the sofa). She stretches out her body and rolls over to expose her tummy. "Whoa! I don't usually move this fast. Maybe we can chat first? What's your sun sign?"

I pretend she answers as Zelda, whose sun sign I already know due to her character trait sheet. "Sagittarius? According to the astrology experts, we are highly compatible then."

I swear to God Sprite winks at me. With the left eye, like Zelda does. Not gonna lie: it kinda freaks me out. I remove the oxygen pin from Sprite's collar and hide it in my dresser.

"Okay, Sprite. It's time for you to go." I pick her up and carry her over to Cathy's. She climbs the hedge and the window scrapes open to allow her entry before slamming down to keep all the illegal felines from making a great escape.

I must be severely lonely if I've resorted to pretending a cat is my crush. I wish I could talk to Finn. Even though I've clicked with Mandy and had fun with her today, that friendship is too new to be as deep as what I had with Finn.

And of course, whenever I find myself missing Finn, I end up wondering how he ended up on the Termination Train without a word of warning. It simply does not make sense to me, and I don't think it ever will.

CHAPTER 13

Even though it's purged from the system, I still have an old, worn copy of Finn's character trait sheet. I pull it out when I miss him too much, like I clearly do today.

Name: Finn

Trope: Manic Pixie Dream Boy (sub-type of Manic Pixie Dream Girl)

Age: 18

Birthday: October 10, Libra

General physical description: Of average build but appears to take up more space because of never staying still, enviably wavy hair in a natural shade of russet, rare heterochromial combination of one dark brown eye and one light blue eye. Basically, hot—but in a non-threatening way.

Clothing style: Follows fads, but will always be partial to pinstripes.

Hobbies: Model trains, breakdancing while pontificating on the benefits of keeping your scalp a shampoo-free zone, photography.

Talents: Puns, poker face, five-time TropeTown air hockey champion.

Strongest positive personality traits: Solution oriented, persuasive, clever.

Strongest negative personality traits: Impulsive, unreliable, self-indulgent.

Ambitions: Truth in all things.

Life philosophy: If you can dream it, you can do it

Favorite foods: Finger foods such as mini-corn dogs or crab puffs or bacon-wrapped dates.

Phobias: FOMO (Fear of Missing Out).

CHAPTER 14

I thank my lucky constellations, Orion and Cassiopeia, when I bump into Zelda the next morning outside the Healing Center. She's wearing her yellow shirt with the periodic square, like the day we met, and I wish I still had the oxygen pin in my pocket. Because then I could present it to her like a geek merit badge and tell her that oxygen is her element because I need her to breathe. On second thought, perhaps it's a blessing I don't have it.

"What's up?" she asks as we get into the empty elevator together. She beats me to hitting our floor button, but our hands brush against each other, and so much electricity sparks between us that she must feel it, too.

Somehow I manage to speak. "My new job started yesterday."

"Ah! I hoped I might see you at the pool hall."

I swoon. She missed me? She sure didn't act like it yesterday. "Did you?"

"Yeah, I'd enjoy running the table on you." She smirks and I don't even mind.

"Next time," I say, but the words kind of get stuck in my throat, and this weird look passes over her face. I can't tell what it's supposed to mean, but it makes me insecure, and I'm not someone who gets insecure about girls.

"Sure," she says, and it's almost as if we're making a date.

"How many more days do you have to attend therapy?" I hope she doesn't notice that I stand unnaturally still.

"Hmmm . . ." She rubs the tendrils on the nape of her neck. "I've lost count. Maybe ten days?"

Ten days. I can wait ten days.

"But therapy is kind of fun, don't you think?" She takes a step closer to me. "Especially with you there."

The elevator doors pick the worst moment ever to open, and Zelda steps away from me. I follow her into the hallway, wishing I were brave enough to take her hand.

"The pie is good, too," I say stupidly, further ruining the moment. "Usually."

She laughs. "Maybe I'll pull a Nebraska and keep coming forever."

"The pie is not *that* good."

"Shh! The Council could be listening. You don't want them to hear you insulting the refreshments."

I can't actually tell if she's joking. She seems to think the Council is constantly eavesdropping on our conversations and divining our innermost thoughts. She might be considered paranoid, but she might also be right.

"C'mon!" She grabs my hand and we skip the rest of the way down the hallway, giggling and out of breath by the time we get there. It's a perfect Manic Pixie Dream sequence. And it's totally real.

CHAPTER 15

Zelda and I enter a full room. In lieu of chairs, Angela has placed pillows on the floor, creating a more intimate atmosphere.

We take the two remaining pillows while Angela passes around a handout, and I set the sheet of paper on my lap. I skim it until I see the rule about not dating anyone in-group while in the group. I wish I could cross it out with a big black marker. They say patience is a virtue, but it sure is a bummer, too.

"As I mentioned yesterday, some of you"—Angela pointedly looks at Nebraska before continuing—"need a refresher concerning the rules of group therapy. I realize your short attention spans might have prevented you from reading the giant binder I issued each of you on your first day, so I printed out an executive summary in easy-to-scan bullet points!" Angela pauses, as if she expects our eternal gratitude for doing us such a grand favor. "Okay, so *most* of you are here because the Council mandated it."

Nebraska coughs, and Angela briefly closes her eyes for a meditative moment. The rest of the girls trade knowing glances. Nebraska and Angela are clearly at odds, but why?

Angela continues. "The Council wants you to be able to perform your duties as a Trope to the best of your abilities, and each of you, for some reason, has been unable to do that."

Sky raises one hand and adjusts her giant headphones with the other.

"Thank you, Sky." Angela reaches into a wicker tote bag behind her and pulls out a pink plastic microphone. She passes it to Sky. "From now on, only the person who holds the microphone may speak."

I want to point out that Angela spoke while Sky was holding the microphone, but she probably feels above her own mandates, so I don't.

Sky brings the toy close to her lips and speaks into it as if it's real. "This totally harshes my vibe. It contradicts us as people. Like, Manic Pixies don't conform to society's rules. So instead of putting us in therapy for not conforming, the Council should be awarding us plaques for a job well done. Why threaten us with termination?"

"Stop right there," Angela commands, snatching the microphone from Sky's grasp.

With her perfect posture and giant hair, Angela is an imposing figure. She'd make a great Benevolent Dictator if her counseling gig goes south. "No one on the Council is threatening you. I am here to help you, and we always want to be as kind and as constructive as possible when dealing with each other."

Since Angela gets her work assignments from the Council, like all of us do, it doesn't surprise me she's acting as their mouthpiece. I can't help feeling uneasy about it, though. She wants us to believe she's on our side, but I'm not so sure.

She gives us a moment to read the rules, but other than the no-dating clause, nothing jumps out at me. Be polite. Be honest. Be on time. Don't spend group time having private conversations. Nebraska has probably broken all of these, which might account for Angela's antagonism. But why is Nebraska still around? Does her status as Legacy give her more latitude?

"Great!" Angela over-enunciates. "Riley, why don't you go ahead and give us a little bit of your background before we give the floor over to Zelda."

When the pink microphone reaches my hands, I have a 'boy-in-headlights' moment and overcompensate by waving it around. "Hi. Uh . . . So, I started in bit parts, mostly fan fiction. Then I worked on an obscure project that ended up in the Author's drawer."

Sympathetic groans from the girls. They know the grind.

"So, I luck out and get cast in this great part from a major Author and the book becomes a runaway bestseller. Living the dream and all that. Well, except my character dies from cancer . . ."

Zelda leans over and taps the microphone, and Angela narrows her eyes but doesn't stop her. "Wait—you're Romantic Cancer Boy?" Zelda asks incredulously. "With all your cheesy dialogue printed in bright colors on coffee mugs and pillowcases in Reader World?"

"See, that's the thing. The Author put those words in my mouth. Some of the things I say sound profound and sweet at first glance, but when I unpack those statements, I find them rather problematic."

Zelda bounces a little in her chair. "Exactly!"

I smile at having scored a point with Zelda. "In my subsequent novel, I wanted to speak my own dialogue. The Author wrote me up twice for being too strong-willed."

Angela shakes her head sadly. "What did you learn from this, Riley?"

"The Author is always right."

Angela prods further. "Even concerning dialogue?"

"Including but not limited to dialogue," I quote the handout directly, and cause Zelda to snicker.

"Are you taking this seriously, Riley?" Angela asks. "I hope so. You have a chance for a breakthrough on your emotional journey. Don't fall back on being superficial and snarky when you can be deep and sincere."

Angela has a gift for making me sound like a shallow douche, and I don't appreciate it. "But what if the dialogue is boring or preachy or stilted? Am I just supposed to spout out whatever inane thing the Author comes up with?"

"It's not up to us to make value judgments or question the Author's judgment. Part of embracing your Trope is knowing your place in the story hierarchy. We are creations, not creators, and therefore, when it comes to our work as Tropes, we have no voice of our own. The sooner you can accept that, the better. Can you accept that?"

My impulse is to say 'no' and drop the mic, but Angela's question held a definite note of warning. I nod agreeably. "I will do my best."

"Excellent. I'm proud of you, Riley." Angela takes the microphone back and passes it to Zelda. "Okay. Zelda, you're up. Tell us why you're here."

I sit up straighter on my pillow. I'm eager to learn everything I can about Zelda.

But Zelda bows her head and mumbles. "I asked my Love Interest to meet me Off-Page."

The girls erupt in horrified titters. Meeting Off-Page with Developeds is totally against TropeTown's policies.

And my heart. It shatters. I might as well hang it next to the heart mosaic on my wall at home.

"Because you're really in love with him?" Chloe asks, plucking the question right out of my brain. She doesn't bother with Angela's unwieldy microphone logistics.

Zelda winces and opens her mouth to say something, but Mandy jumps in.

"It's only natural to feel that way!" Mandy exclaims. "That's how you make the Readers believe you're in love, by believing in it yourself."

"I'm not in love with him." Zelda stares at the floor. "That's not the reason I asked."

My sigh of relief releases all the trapped air in my body. I still have a chance with this beautiful, complicated girl.

"But when he refused, he made me feel so insecure. I mean, he's a Developed and I'm just a Trope. He's poetry, and I'm shorthand."

Angela suddenly looks like she just ate something rotten. "That's a tough situation, but he was probably looking out for your best interest by not meeting you Off-Page and then turning you in."

"No, Chet would never turn me in," Zelda insists, cleaning off her glasses with the edge of her T-shirt. "It must have been someone else."

Chet? I get irrationally angry hearing Zelda's Love Interest has such a stupid name. I know I'm not supposed to be making value judgments, but can you blame me?

Nebraska fiddles with all the necklaces she's wearing, and the charms clink together. She couldn't look any more bored if she were dead. Again, why does she keep coming to these sessions when she doesn't have to?

Angela recovers from her unprofessional display of disgust and puts on her most soothing tone. "I don't know why you'd risk meeting anyone Off-Page. But be happy it isn't because you're actually in love with him. Trust me, if you fall for a person"—her voice hardens at the word 'person' and the atmosphere in the room buzzes—"who can't or won't love you back, it can only end in heartbreak."

Zelda juts out her chin. "I want to feel worthy. I want to be taken seriously."

"Rule Number One is . . . ," Angela prompts.

"Embrace your Trope," Zelda intones, clearly not happy about it.

"That's right!" Angela is too cheerful. "Which means accepting your Trope's limitations and understanding some things are simply not possible for you. Now let's meditate on that idea for a few minutes before we end the session, shall we?"

As the girls bow their head in contemplation, these are my thoughts:

1. I need to convince Zelda she's worth everything.
2. I want to kick Chet's backside. How dare he make her feel less than?
3. Pie. Where's the freaking pie?

CHAPTER 16

When the session ends, all I want to do is wrap Zelda in a soothing hug, but she is summoned away by her Author before I have a chance. My thoughts jumble into a mess of insecurities and doubts about what I can possibly offer to someone as self-sufficient as Zelda.

You know how when someone has a crisis of confidence in an animated film, a gray cloud follows them, hovering over their head while everyone else goes about their sunny ways? Even though that isn't literally happening to me, that's exactly how I feel as I walk home. I know I'm being melodramatic, but that's what a powerful semi-unrequited crush can do to you.

When I reach my apartment, a huge lug of a stranger occupies my front step. He looks like he could kick my butt seven times in a minute and a half, and he has a classic cleft in his chin to boot.

When he sees me, his lip curls in a snarl. "Are you Riley?"

I rock backward on my heels. This crappy day is going from Category 1 Pity-Party to Category 5 Existential-Calamity. Did my latest Author make a complaint? Did the Council send this guy to haul me off to the Termination Train?

My immediate instinct is to deny my identity. But before I

can turn and run, his expression wilts and his shoulders droop. "I miss Mandy so damn much."

"Clark?" I try to cover the nervous crack in my voice with a cough. I remind myself I have nothing to fear. After all, Clark can't be an Abusive Jerk. If he were, he'd be confined to the Villain Zone on the Wrong Side of the Tracks. Sensitive Nice Guys have their issues, but they don't beat up the quirky friends of their exes.

He nods miserably. "I need your help, man. To win her back."

Clark has picked the wrong day for a pep talk from this Manic Pixie, but they do say misery loves commiseration. Maybe the universe sent him as support for my serious case of romantic blues, or maybe I'm merely addicted to putting a positive spin on all my predicaments. "Come on in, I guess. Hot chocolate?"

"Yes, please." He perks up slightly and lumbers in after me.

While I head to the kitchen to make our drinks, Clark cannonballs onto my sofa, squeaking it across the wood floor. From my cabinet, I pull down two oversized, white mugs splotched with blue paint like abstract art. While I heat up the milk, I wonder how much I should tell him about my interaction with Mandy. Would she be upset if I betrayed her confidence? Does my loyalty lie with the Manic Pixie Trope, or does the Bro Code trump all? I haven't had a "bro" in my life since Finn, and he's certainly not here to ask.

By the time I return with two mugs full of hot chocolate, Clark is rocking slowly back and forth with his arms hugged tight around himself. "What did I do wrong?" he wails.

I nudge a mug into his hand, and he relaxes. He takes a gulp before I can warn him of the hotness level, but he doesn't even flinch as he swallows.

"I mean . . . you might have gifted her a few too many breakable baubles," I suggest carefully. I stir my drink with the cinnamon stick and breathe in the swirls of rich-smelling steam.

"I thought, because of who she is, Mandy would dig all the whimsical glass stuff." He stumbles over the word "whimsical," like it's something he's trying on to impress, and not a normal part of his vocabulary. "That's why I got a job at the glass factory."

To get a service job, Clark must have petitioned for a hiatus from Trope duties. He scores points for dedication at least.

Clark downs the rest of his hot chocolate and presses his empty mug into my side. "More, please."

"Here." I didn't make enough for seconds, so I give him my portion. I instantly regret being such a generous person. "Maybe it's time to move on," I suggest.

"But I love glass. And I love Mandy."

"Dude, learn moderation," I say. "Two grasshoppers are cute, one hundred grasshoppers constitute a plague."

He scrunches his forehead. "What do grasshoppers have to do with anything?"

I sigh. "Nothing. Just lay off the glass. That's my advice."

"If I do, will she take me back?"

I hesitate. Mandy seemed adamant about being done with Clark. But if his figurine fixation is the only major deal breaker, perhaps if he could get over that she might reconsider. Despite the infusion of cocoa goodness, Clark looks as lost as a lovesick puppy, so my sympathetic nature leads me to root for him.

While I'm trying to decide how to respond, Clark seems to notice his surroundings for the first time. "Wait a minute." He gets up and approaches my heart mosaic. "Where'd you get this broken glass?"

"Uh . . ." There are people who say honesty is the best policy, but those people have probably never had to face down a 250-pound glass aficionado on a formidable sugar high. "Found it?"

Clark scrutinizes it further. "This looks like . . . part of a claw. And this looks like part of a tail fin. My lobsters! My precious lobsters!"

He stands there, six plus feet of bewildered betrayal, a victim of our free-spirited vandalism. I don't regret having smashed the lobsters, but I regret getting caught with the evidence.

"I'm sorry," I venture, trying to make it at least sound semi-sincere. I mean, he can always make new lobsters. Dude obviously loves blowing the glass.

He wipes at one of his eyes, like he might cry. "Brutal, man. How could you do it?"

"It wasn't exactly *my* idea," I blurt.

Clark reacts like I've punched him in face. "Mandy?" he asks in a small voice. I feel like the slimiest worm on the sidewalk after a flash flood. And I just got stepped on.

I avoid his gaze. Darn it. I don't want to rat Mandy out more than I have already. She's my friend, and as much as I might sympathize with Clark, I'm still going to side with her. If she doesn't want to be with him, then she shouldn't be with him.

He sits down on my sofa and buries his head in his hands. "I just want to make her happy."

"Uh, have you ever considered the best way to make her happy right now is to leave her alone and move on with your life?"

His reply consists of muffled sniffles and gasps. I'm not sure what to do. Should I comfort him? It's always awkward to watch someone you barely know cry. Especially when you're partially responsible for it.

I retrieve a box of tissues. I perch next to him and pat him on his heaving back. "Thought you might want these."

He glances up with red, puffy eyes, recognizes the tissues, and snatches a handful to wipe at his cheeks. Finally he says, "What if someone gave you that advice about the girl you loved? Could you do it? Move on without giving it your all? Could you live with yourself, wondering if there were something more you could have done, and you just gave up?"

I don't think my situation with Zelda warrants such desperate musings just yet. "Dude, this has nothing to do with me. Go talk to Mandy."

"So you do think it might make her happy to talk to me?" His face shines with both tears and hope.

If I tell him what I really think, he's never, ever going to leave my sofa.

"How will you know," I say, resigned, "if you don't give it your all?"

CHAPTER 17

After Clark leaves, my Author summons me.

I land disoriented per usual and stumble over to the craft services table. After imbibing four bottles of water, I take a moment to note the paltry nature of today's spread. There's only a half-eaten bowl of meatballs and a tiny bowl of multi-colored mints. What the hell?

"Hello Marsden." Ava comes up behind me. "There used to be more food, but the Author wrote a crowd scene earlier and the Extras descended upon our feast like wild ferrets."

I can tell by her more playful word choice I'm already rubbing off on her. It's often like this with burgeoning characters. They start with such basic personalities that they take on other voices before they finally grow secure in their own. Sometimes that doesn't happen until the later revision stages. I don't mind, though. It's flattering to have an influence, even it if it's ephemeral.

"Oh, you've been doing scenes without me?"

There's a twinkle in Ava's eye that wasn't there before. Also, her hair is down, and it doesn't look like she combed it. "Yes. In fact, I found out my inciting incident. My boyfriend broke up with me because I'm only going to be a senior in high school and he's off to college and doesn't want to be tied down."

So I was right on that count. "That's rough."

"But when he sees me with you, he decides he wants me back."

I groan. "Not another love triangle!"

She laughs and licks her lower lip. "It's not the worst thing in the world. Especially because the Author is skipping ahead to writing the kissing scenes, and I decided I really like kissing."

She's peering up at me between thick lashes in a way that makes me simultaneously blush and squirm.

"That's cool." It's not cool though, because I don't want to kiss Ava. I get a pang in my chest. Zelda is probably kissing Chet right now, and maybe even enjoying it.

"Rafferty—that's my ex-boyfriend—has been helping me practice Off-Page too."

"Ahhh." I'm intrigued by this, though not for the reason Ava might think. I've never really considered how and where Developeds live while their Author writes their book. But obviously they have to live somewhere Off-Page until the world of the Novel is fully built, and I guess it makes sense they would all hang out, like we do. Though their community is much smaller. And what if a book only has one Developed? Does that lonely soul live like a hermit?

Before I can ask Ava about her life Off-Page, the green light goes on over the stage door, and Ava grabs my hand and tugs me along with her.

The Author types out our scene like a screenplay, a writing tactic useful for first drafting.

MARSDEN: I looked for you at the game last night.

AVA (averts her eyes): I . . . I didn't feel like going.

MARSDEN: Not enough pep in your step for the epic pre-season battle between our hometown heroes and their most vilified opponents?

AVA: When you put it that way—I really didn't feel like going.

MARSDEN: Not a football fan, eh? Can't say I blame you.

AVA: I went to all the games last year. When Rafferty was starting quarterback.

MARSDEN: Oh. (Awkward pause) Well, our hometown heroes lost. Whoever is playing quarterback now took a beating.

AVA: I heard. Maybe he'll get better by the time school starts and the games actually count.

MARSDEN: Maybe. But I don't actually want to talk about football.

AVA: You don't?

MARSDEN: You want to go for a walk?

Oh real smooth, Marsden. Everyone knows "You want to go for walk?" is code for "You want to go somewhere and make out?" It's painful to not protest this dialogue. Would Angela give me a rainbow star if she could see how well I am deferring to the wishes of the Author, however inane they are? (Sorry, value judgment. Couldn't help it.)

AVA (shrugs): Okay.

MARSDEN: Did you feel that?

AVA: Raindrops.

MARSDEN: An unexpected pleasure.

AVA: What? You like getting rained on?

MARSDEN (brushes Ava's hair behind her shoulder): I like kissing in the rain.

AVA (shivers): You do?

MARSDEN: I do.

So at this point, I'm supposed to go in for the kiss. Ava closes her eyes, waiting, and my body screams at me to abort, but my head tells me I'd better follow the script.

Ava's soft lips make the kiss pleasant, but I'm thinking too much. Where should I put my hands? Is this too much tongue? Should I turn my head to the right? Would that eliminate the crick in my neck? Is she enjoying this?

By setting this scene in the rain, the Author is clearly going for passionate abandon, but I don't feel it, and I doubt my actions are going to translate well to the page. I pull away.

The green light goes out, indicating the Author has finished with us for now.

"What's wrong?" Ava asks once we're off-stage.

I spear one of the meatballs with a toothpick. "Nothing."

"Are you jealous I was with Rafferty?"

"You mean, instead of at the game last night?"

She smiles. "You picked up on that subtext, did you?"

"This isn't my first novel, darling."

"He's a better kisser than you are."

I know I shouldn't care, because I don't want Ava anyway and thus I have zero investment in her opinion, but it still rankles. Manic Pixies may seem chill, but we actually have a pretty strong competitive streak when challenged.

"We're just getting started," I say with a wink. "Seems premature of you to make a decision already."

"We'll see." She pulls her hair back into a ponytail and smoothes it out with her fingers. "The Author says you can go."

I shouldn't read into the Author sending me home in the middle of a scene—Authors do it all the time for a variety of reasons—but it leaves me with an uneasy feeling. I vow to be more engaged next time.

I need this Author to like me. At least enough not to officially complain about me.

CHAPTER 18

When I land back on my sofa, it takes me a few moments to discern that the scratching sound I hear is not part of the low-grade headache I always get after jumping back to Trope-Town, but is actually coming from the front door. I peer out my peephole to investigate, but I don't see anything out of the ordinary.

The scratching grows more urgent, so I open the door. Sprite sits there looking like the cat that ate Big Bird.

"What is it, Sprite?"

She turns and flounces away.

I shake my head, and I am about to shut the door when I notice a sparkle of silver on the white concrete that Sprite vacated. A pin. With Ag-47, the symbol for silver, printed on it. Attached to a folded note card. I open it.

Meet me at our bridge. −Z

Not knowing how long ago Zelda left this for me, I spring into action. I don't want to miss her, but I don't want to show up looking like a slob either. So I run back to my closet, which is full of the clothes that came with my character. I have them organized by color, and my hand reaches for a pale yellow polo shirt I've never worn before. I know Zelda likes yellow. I also pull on a pair of gray skinny jeans, a gray scarf, and a gray hoodie. And yellow baseball cleats, just because.

It's not until I'm at the edge of Seasons Park that I let myself do a full-on internal happy dance—my heart and my lungs spinning in anticipation. Zelda asked to meet me!

When I get to "our" bridge, she is sitting with her legs dangling in the water, her heeled boots and socks in a pile behind her. Clips that look like wings adorn her hair, giving the impression she's about to take flight. She has a book open on her lap, and the ducks float in a semi-circle around her as if listening attentively.

She greets me without even glancing back.

"Hey, Riley. Hope you brought your crackers. Our illustrious audience demands snacks!"

Strike one.

"Sorry, ducks," I call out. "Better luck next time!"

They quack their disappointment and swim away.

"How did you get all your ducks lined up in a row?" I ask Zelda.

She rolls her eyes at my poor pun attempt. "They aren't my ducks. If they were my ducks, I'd dress them up in tiny duck tuxedo jackets and take them to the opera."

"You should be empress of the entire Anatidae family." I tap her on the head with my imaginary scepter.

She bows her head as if to accept her coronation. "It's generous of you to include the geese and swans in my empire."

"I would gladly give you so much more."

Zelda raises an eyebrow but doesn't comment. She closes the book on her lap and holds out her hand.

I help her up, and she slides her wet feet into her boots and tucks her socks into the breast pocket of her blazer. It looks stylish and intentional, which shouldn't surprise me, but it does—a good indicator I'm feeling off-balance.

"I want to go ice skating," she declares.

"Then ice skating you shall go."

"You can't ice skate in baseball cleats," she points out.

"Maybe we should play baseball instead," I tease as we start walking in the direction of Winter Lake.

"Never. It's way too boring."

"Well, baseball is far less boring than, say, waiting for pasta to boil."

"That's a false equivalency."

"That reminds me of something Finn once said to me," I say. "Shortly before he boarded the Termination Train."

She stops so suddenly that my peripheral vision suffers whiplash. And when I turn around to look at her, she has this split-second terrified expression before she covers it with a nervous smile. "We shouldn't talk about that," she says, almost inaudibly, through clenched teeth.

Strike two?

Zelda is staring at me hard, like she's trying to telepathically tell me something of extreme importance but I'm too dense to get it.

Nevertheless, I decide to finish my original thought. "All Finn said was, 'Remember, Riley, you always have a choice.' So I am choosing to equate baseball with pasta."

She heaves a mock sigh but seems to appreciate that I've steered the conversation away from termination. "So, if I give you that, I can still say I think pasta is less boring."

"You can." I also mock sigh, while grinning with relief that

I haven't chased her away. "But then you have to defend your position."

"While waiting for pasta to boil . . ." she makes a gesture like she's dipping her fork into the pot on the stove, ". . . you can extract noodles and throw them at the wall until they stick."

"Am I to assume from your defense that you have a collage of dried spaghetti over your stove?"

She twirls and begins to run through a field of sunflowers. "Maybe you'll find out one of these days."

CHAPTER 19

By the time we reach Winter Lake, it's twilight. Deep shades of purple and blue pour out of the sky and onto the frozen surface beneath our feet. Icicles dangle from the branches of the tall pine trees that surround the perfect oval of the lake. We don't have skates, but Zelda holds onto me as she slides around in her boots. My cleats sink down and keep us grounded. I won't let us fall.

Eventually she tires of swirling and spinning around me, and she stands motionless, still clutching my collar. It's not as cold as real winter, but a crisp wind chills the air, and our breath comes out in wisps. I unwind my scarf from around my neck and wrap it around hers.

"Thank you," she says. She pulls her socks from her blazer pocket and puts them on like mittens. "Snow angels?"

We lie down on the ice close enough to huddle for warmth, which is too close, we both realize at once, to be separate angels. Her face rests inches from mine, her hair dusted with snowflakes and already curling at the ends.

"We'll just have to be one giant angel," I say. "I'll follow your lead."

I extend my left arm and she extends her right and I mimic

her swishing motion exactly. After a minute, she props herself up on one elbow to survey our progress. "There's not enough snow to really leave our mark."

I turn over and lift myself into a kneeling position and pull off one of my cleats. I use the most forward spike as a writing implement, and I scrawl out a message: *WE WERE HERE.*

Zelda kneels beside me and takes the cleat when I'm finished. "We have to sign our names, too." She writes her name in a flowery cursive and adds the plus sign underneath it. "Now you."

Her sock mittens brush against my palm as she returns my cleat. I shiver and my signature comes out looking somewhat shaky.

But it's there. We are both linked to this moment in time. To this place. To each other. No one can take this from us. Not the TropeTown Council. Not our Authors. Not our Readers.

Zelda nods her approval and tackles me, reaching up under my shirt to tickle the bare skin of my sides. I freeze up because it feels amazing, but I don't know what it means. Normally if a girl touches me like this, it's because she has a crush on me, but Zelda froze me out just this morning, so I can't be sure.

I'm used to being unflappable, to reading signals and responding the right way every time. It's in my DNA, you might say. But Zelda is a riddle, wrapped in a mystery, inside a Manic Pixie Dream Girl exterior.

Her fingers stop twitching and her socked hands press against me, one on my chest and the other on the small of my back. She cuddles closer but her eyes gaze upwards. We lie here, still. As the companionable silence stretches out, I smile at the thought of our quirky chemistry.

"Do you ever look at this sky," Zelda asks, "and wonder if it's the same sky Readers see?"

"You mean . . . are we all connected somehow?"

"Yeah." She shifts her weight and has maybe turned her head to look at me, but I'm so paralyzed by never wanting her to move her body away that I keep staring straight up. On this clear night, the lights of the city seem far away, and the stars dot the darkness like a colony of albino ants.

"I have to believe we are. I have to believe we matter." The cold from the ice seeps into the parts of me that Zelda doesn't warm.

She sighs. "The Developeds are the ones who get to touch people's lives. They have the important storylines and the resonant scenes."

"Yeah, but you know we play an integral part, too, otherwise we wouldn't even exist."

Even as I say it, an uncomfortable thought strikes me. I've been basking in the classic Manic Pixie dreaminess of my interactions with Zelda, but maybe it only feels special because everything our Trope does is *supposed* to seem special. How much of how we act is pre-programmed for maximum Manic Pixie normativity? And how much free will do we really have?

"I want to exist for more than just convenience." Zelda's voice trembles. "I'm tired of playing the part expected of me just to keep everyone else happy. What about my happiness? Doesn't that count for something?"

"It does to me," I whisper.

She doesn't respond. I'm pretty sure she didn't hear me. Her teeth are chattering. She'll get sick if we stay out here any longer.

"It's cold, and we aren't dressed properly." I reluctantly extricate myself from her embrace, but before I can get up, she grips me by the shoulders and looks me straight in the eye.

"I have such a good time with you, Riley."

She kisses me.

On the forehead.

It may not be what I hoped for, but it's a start. So maybe I won't strike out after all.

CHAPTER 20

Zelda isn't at therapy the next morning. I miss her and her smirks and even her mixed signals.

Sky takes her turn at the mic today, and though I can hardly be blamed for not paying rapt attention due to Zelda never leaving my thoughts, I catch the salient points of her story. She rallied the supporting characters in her last novel to create their own subplot where Sky's character puts on an epic battle of the bands. Unfortunately, it was a Very Serious Book about a Very Serious Issue, and the Author complained that Sky's fun and frivolous meanderings clashed tonally with the rest.

"And I think instead of excising the *good* parts, the Author should have aspired to amp up his boring stuff," Sky grumbles, squeezing her fist around the base of Angela's pink microphone so tightly, it looks like she might warp the plastic. "I hope he ends up remaindered. Or pulped."

Everyone gasps. Even me.

Angela recovers quickly from her shock. "I would like you to try to rephrase your statements to be more positive, please."

"Why?" Sky asks. "It's not like the Author listens in, right? That's what you always *claim*, anyway."

"Our goal here is to remember our place," Angela says

patiently, though I notice an eyelid twitch. "We are subject to the Author's vision. And the Author is always right."

"The Author is always right," we all drone, expect for Sky. She and Angela stare each other down until Sky finally relents.

"Fine," Sky says, slumping in her chair and letting the mic drop into her lap. "The Author is always right."

Angela beams. "Very good, Sky!"

"Still." Sky closes her hand loosely around the mic. "It's a shame that subplot had to go. It was so cool."

"You remember it," I blurt. "Tell us about it, and we'll remember it with you."

Fortunately, Angela doesn't chastise me for speaking out of turn. In fact, she supports me. "What an excellent idea, Riley. Let's serve the pie and have a story hour!"

No complaints from me on that count. I cut the pie, a lemon meringue, and everyone takes a piece except for Nebraska, who waves me away waggling her fingers. Mandy grabs a plate from me a little too roughly and mutters a 'thank you' without meeting my eyes. Her lips are set in such a thin line, I can barely make out her trademark red lipstick.

But I quickly forget about her brusqueness as I get lost in Sky's story and the spellbinding cadence of her words. I admire the way she threw herself into her character, the way she left an echo of her true self in the story.

But is that the best we can hope for? To give pieces of ourselves to the characters we play until we become empty caricatures of ourselves? Maybe that explains why Nebraska is so sharp-edged and bitter. Would her personality have developed differently if she had the chance to control her own story?

When the session ends and we all go our separate ways, Mandy confronts me in the elevator. "I'm mad at you."

One guess to why she might be upset. "Did Clark visit you?"

"Yes. And he gifted me two glass grasshoppers." Mandy pulls a pink paper box out of her bag, and she opens it to show me two perfectly formed green grasshoppers. "He said you told him to!"

I whistle in appreciation for his glassblowing, skills far superior to his intellectual capability. "Clark is quite the talent, though."

"He is, isn't he?" A proud smile breaks through her frustration for a moment. "But that does not get you off the hook."

"I'm sorry. Clark completely misunderstood my advice on the grasshopper front, but I did tell him he should work out his problems directly with you instead of trying to use me as a middleman."

"He sat on my sofa and stared at my mosaic for, like, ten minutes." Mandy huffs. "And then burst into sobs."

I can imagine this scene perfectly. Clark breaking down and Mandy comforting him, making him false promises of eternal glass adoration she cannot possibly keep. "So you got back together?"

She throws up her arms in a gesture of defeat. "How could we not? I'm not a heartless beast."

Would the sobbing tactic work on Zelda? I doubt it. For starters, we don't have the history Mandy and Clark share—we can't get back together when we've never been a couple. Plus, I'm not prone to sobbing. Minor welling and tearing up, here and there, but no major waterworks.

"Do you love him, though?"

"I want to," she answers. "And some days I think I could. Isn't that enough? For now?"

Judging from Mandy's pained expression, I would say 'no,'

but haven't I already meddled enough? Relationships sure are tough to navigate when there is no Author controlling the outcome.

"Look, I'm the wrong person to ask for relationship advice." And when I say it, my voice wobbles.

"Riley has a crush on someone." Mandy sing-songs this statement, as if I'm a kindergartener about to develop a terminal case of cooties. "And I know who it is."

To my relief, the elevator door opens, offering me an escape route. "No, you don't."

"Please." Her tone becomes serious as she trails me out of the elevator. "I've noticed the way you look at Zelda."

The blush rampaging across my face confirms Mandy's suspicions. Betrayed by my own body! "I don't think she looks at me the same way," I confess.

Mandy gives me a long, consoling hug. She must agree with my assessment, which makes me even more insecure than I already am.

"Zelda has a lot going on. Maybe romance is not a priority for her at the moment."

Ouch. Is Mandy implying that *my* priorities are screwed up? "Well, maybe it *would* be her priority if there weren't the whole therapy non-fraternization rule to consider," I point out.

"But see, here's the thing. Even if it weren't against the therapy rules—when have you ever heard of two Manic Pixies in love? I mean, wouldn't the universe explode from an overload of quirky cuteness? It's probably better for our continued existence that you leave her to all her admirers at the pool hall."

"You play pool with her?" I must sound accusatory, because she gets defensive.

"Yeah, and you could, too, if you ever went out with us."

"You've never invited me out."

She scrunches up her features in confusion, as if including me in all the Manic Pixie group activities had never occurred to her before. "You're welcome to come whenever. I won't be there tonight because I have a date with Clark, but I know Zelda and some others are going. The pool hall has been a popular Manic Pixie meet-up spot for eons."

My mind immediately jumps ahead to what I'll say to Zelda at the pool hall. Will I feign disinterest, or will her charm disarm me?

"Can you not tell anyone about my feelings for Zelda?"

Mandy laughs. "Sure, as long as you refrain from encouraging Clark to give me more grasshoppers."

"If only he'd listen," I sigh. But we shake on it.

CHAPTER 21

I barely make it inside my apartment before my Author summons button glows. I groan, even though working might help distract me from obsessing over Zelda.

When I land, Ava stands waiting for me with a tall glass of tomato juice. Thanks to my excessive thirst, I don't even care that tomato juice makes me want to vomit.

"An Inspiring Teacher Trope did a scene with me earlier," Ava says as I gratefully chug the brackish beverage, trying not to engage my taste buds. "She explained that tomato juice provides the most effective electrolyte replacement after a jump so you can perform at your highest level."

"I appreciate your concern." She can't know a Developed has never served me anything before, and I don't want to unsettle her with an over-the-top reaction to her kindness.

"Well, maybe I could've been nicer to you these past couple of days, Riley."

Both her sincerity and her use of my actual name floor me. She takes the empty glass from my hand and returns it to the craft services table, which is lucky because otherwise I might have dropped the glass in shock. I follow her over to the table and dig into a bowl of jelly beans to cleanse my palate.

"I want our scenes to keep Readers up at night," she continues. "I want them to engage in passionate discussions about whether Ava should be with Marsden or with Rafferty. And for that to happen, I need to be invested. And so do you."

This sounds to me like the Author talking, but I don't want to offend her by suggesting as much. "Whose team are you on? Team Marsden or Team Rafferty?"

Ava ponders this. "The Author hasn't figured that out yet."

"Your choice in a love triangle depends on who *you* want to be," I say, like I'm imparting some sacred literary wisdom, instead of something Finn once told me while roasting marshmallows. "If you choose Rafferty, you're saying you can't stop clinging to the past, while choosing Marsden means you're embracing your future."

"That sounds incredibly biased," Ava says, but there's a teasing note in her voice so I know she's not upset. "Maybe it'll all come down to who kisses the best. So prepare to pucker up!"

I blow her a kiss.

"Oh, you want to practice a bit before we go on set?" She shuffles her feet and won't look at me. Out of shyness? Reluctance? How do I keep landing in mixed-signal city? Not that it matters in this case.

"It feels more genuine if it arises in the moment," I say, diplomatically. And to lessen the tension, I throw a pair of green jelly beans at her.

"Hey!" she protests, and loads up on her own candy ammunition, which obviously leads us down the slippery slope of food fighting. It may start with innocent intentions, but it always ends with a face full of frosting, doesn't it?

I do a mental comparison of the Ava I first met and the Ava who stands before me now. She still defaults to prim, but I can't imagine the Ava of a few days ago happily licking cake off the sides of her mouth. It's endearing.

A Burly Stagehand enters with a broom. He shakes his head at us while he sweeps.

"I'm surprised the Author hasn't called us in yet," Ava says as we dust the crumbs off our clothes and apply towels to the gunk on our skin.

"You have a chocolate sprinkle on your earlobe." I lean in with my mouth open as if I'm going to bite the sprinkle away, but as she turns her head her nose bangs into my chin. We both startle and back off to give each other space. *Awkward.*

She drifts over to her chair, and I watch the Burly Stagehand wipe down the craft services table. All traces of our fun disappear as if they never existed.

Finally, we get the green light for the day's work. Our wardrobe appears on the rack. I have to wear a pair of camo-printed galoshes and Ava gets a red jacket with a hood.

The Author begins to revise the scene we did yesterday. She starts by adding setting details, so that instead of occupying a blank space, Ava and I are now crouched below the bleachers as fat raindrops splatter and plunk on the metal above our heads.

The Author describes the freshly mown grass of the football field, the darkening sky of dusk, and the faraway drone of the cars on the highway beyond the school until it all comes to life around us. I put everything else out of my head and allow myself to be present in the moment. No analyzing the Author's choices, just feeling the words she types flow through me.

Ava zips up her jacket and pulls on the hood so it casts shadows on her face. "Rain, rain, go away."

"Don't you mean: rain, rain, please stay?" I say.

"Why? You like getting rained on?"

Her hood is wide and loose, and I tuck a stray strand of her hair behind her ear. "I like kissing in the rain."

She shivers and her voice goes all husky and low. "You do?"

"I do."

Lightning strikes somewhere close, illuminating her parted lips and curious eyes. Thunder shakes the concrete beneath us. We kiss, and we're so caught up in it we barely notice it has started to pour.

When we finally break apart, my feet are the only dry part on my body.

Ava makes fun of my drowned-fox appearance, and I grab her hand, and we run all the way to her house, only stopping once we get to her porch.

"Thanks for getting me home safely, Marsden." She grins. "And thanks for introducing me to the positive side of rain. I'm sold."

"Keep checking the weather forecast," I joke, "and we'll meet up for the next storm."

The television blares from the living room, and pots and pans clang together in the kitchen. "I have to go inside now," she says, though she seems reluctant to do so. "But don't catch a cold. I want to see you tomorrow."

"Even if the sun shines?"

"Even then." She slips through her door and shuts it behind her.

And . . . end of scene.

The setting disappears, and Ava and I once again occupy a bare stage.

I've journeyed so deeply inside of Marsden's skin, I have to close my eyes for a few seconds and take a deep breath to reset.

"Wow." Ava puts her hand over her heart. "Go Team Marsden!"

We walk backstage together.

"So are you going to petition the Author for more kissing scenes, then?" I tease.

She hangs up her drenched jacket. "Even if the sun shines."

CHAPTER 22

I make my way to the pool hall, riding the particular high produced by a successful creative session. Appropriate, since the Recreational District hollers with fun. I bounce down the rubberized road, and along the way, Carnival Workers try to lure me to test my strength or ride a zip-line or swim in a giant vat of plastic balls.

But I won't be swayed from my mission to see Zelda tonight, even if I won't exactly advertise that I kissed another girl. Granted, I only did it because it's my job, but the twinge of guilt stems from the fact that I enjoyed it—though that's my job, too.

The pool hall occupies the basement of the Wild West Saloon, so I have to squeeze my way through a crowd of leather-vested revelers cheering on those brave enough to mount the mechanical bull. Peanut shells crackle under my feet and yee-haws bounce off the walls. I thud down the stairs into the dim light of the pool hall, happy to escape the full-on assault on my senses.

I scan the tables, my heart beating in pace with the frenetic line dancing upstairs. Zelda isn't here, but I spy Nebraska, holding court at a corner table. She sits regally on a red barstool that matches her hair dye, and when she looks over and recognizes me, she beckons me to come over.

"You may go," she says to the two guys playing in front of her. Without a word, they abandon their game. They rack up their cues, but leave their balls behind.

There's nowhere else to sit, and Nebraska doesn't seem in any hurry to abdicate her throne, so I stand awkwardly beside her, shoving my hands in my pockets. "Come here often?" I say, my tongue firmly in my cheek. This line couldn't be any cheesier unless you fried it in cheddar.

"I do not frequent this establishment, no."

I raise my eyebrow. I almost ask her where the rest of the Manic Pixie club is, but it doesn't seem like the best tactical move, so I wait for her to speak again.

"You know, Finn used to come over to my place to play pool," she says finally. "Quite often actually."

I try to hide my shock, but she's too savvy.

"Oh my, he never told you, did he?" She bares her teeth in a facsimile of a smile and pats my shoulder. "And you were his *best friend* and everything."

"He never talked about you at all." I mean it as a slam, to insinuate that she wasn't important enough to be a topic of conversation, but if it bothers her, you'd never know it by looking at her. How did a Manic Pixie become such an Ice Queen Diva? I'm surprised the Council hasn't transferred her Trope allegiance.

She points at the formation of balls on the felt. "You're behind the eight ball like he was."

I start to get a very bad feeling. "What do you mean?"

"Finn also fell in love with a fellow Manic Pixie."

I want to protest, but no words come out. What can I say,

anyway? Apparently I'm so obvious about my crush on Zelda that even Nebraska has cared to notice. So instead I ask the obvious question. "Who was Finn in love with?"

As far as I know, Finn spent most of his time either working or hanging out with me, and we rarely talked about girls, except in relation to our current projects.

Nebraska fans herself with the feathers of her peacock shawl. "With *me*, dummy," she says.

"No way." If that's true, I really didn't know Finn at all.

"He wrote me enough love letters to fill a slew of hatboxes. He asked me to shred and scatter them after I read them, and I honored his wishes."

I feel woozy. I sit down on the floor, and some gelatinous substance sticks to my jeans. From this angle, I can see up Nebraska's appealingly upturned nose.

"But that's not the point," she continues. "The point is you're playing a dangerous game, and as a friend, I'm advising you to be careful. You know very well what happened to dear Finn."

Except I don't. At least, I have no idea why he was terminated. Is Nebraska implying Finn's alleged crush on her led to his untimely demise?

Before I can ask her to clarify, Nebraska hops off her stool and saunters away.

I stay seated on the floor, my mind racing. Manic Pixies aren't explicitly forbidden to date unless they are in therapy together, are they? Though I suppose if Finn hid a relationship with Nebraska from me, he could have also hidden a stint in group therapy . . .

But there's a more chilling implication: maybe it will never be safe for me to date Zelda. Like Mandy said earlier, maybe

Manic Pixies simply aren't made for one another, and the TropeTown authorities will intervene at some point.

I'm no longer up for playing pool. I don't even want to wait for the others to arrive or to see Zelda. I get up and walk out without a backward glance.

CHAPTER 23

Naturally my encounter with Nebraska made me curious enough to look up her character trait sheet.

Name: Nebraska
Trope: Manic Pixie Dream Girl
Age: 19
Birthday: October 29, Scorpio
General physical description: Willowy. Blue eyes. Choppy blond hair, dipped in red. The perfect nose (a 106-degree angle upward rotation measured from the lip). Basically, hot—but in a non-threatening way.
Clothing style: Tends towards the bombastic and eccentric. Mixes high-end designer pieces with thrift-store finds. Would never be caught dead in sweatpants.
Hobbies: Trapeze, drag racing, cross-pollenating tomatoes.
Talents: Inappropriately morbid jokes, speed reading, a photographic memory, can juggle and hula hoop at the same time.
Strongest positive personality traits: Determined, ambitious, and passionate.

Strongest negative personality traits: Manipulative, easily bored, and resentful. Also drinks too much, often by herself.

Ambitions: Be the best at being bubbly.

Life philosophy: You can never truly know anyone, not even yourself.

Favorite foods: Potato chips dipped in caviar.

Phobias: Irrelevance.

CHAPTER 24

"Guess who got a job?" Chloe squeals the next day in therapy. While I privately lament Zelda's absence, Chloe does her signature freaky dance. We are all moved to join her, even Nebraska. In fact, Nebraska imitates Chloe so well, she could *be* Chloe.

Angela indulges us for a minute before making us sit down. "Why don't you tell us about it, Chloe?"

"Uh . . . I'd rather not go into details . . ."

"OMG! It's dinosaur erotica, isn't it?" George says.

"No!"

"A musical opus conceived as a fifth-grade class project?" Sky guesses.

"No."

"A post-apocalyptic vision commissioned and computer-generated by our new Robot Overlords?" I joke.

Chloe crosses her eyes and sticks out her lower lip. "Stop. It," she says in a zany robot voice. "I'll. Never. Tell."

"Well, congratulations," Nebraska purrs. "I'm sure whatever you've been hired to do befits your talent." It's amazing how sincere Nebraska sounds, even though I'm sure she means this as an insult.

Chloe goes completely still, so I can tell she feels the devastating impact of Nebraska's velvet sledgehammer. She can't call Nebraska on it, though, because Nebraska has plausible deniability on her side. She could argue Chloe is paranoid or doesn't know how to accept a compliment.

I loosen my collar. The air barely circulates due to the tightly latched window. I detect notes of vanilla and brown sugar wafting from the pie table.

Angela swiftly changes the subject. "So, today we're giving the microphone to Georgina." At the use of George's real name, Nebraska snickers.

"George," George corrects.

"Go ahead, George," Angela says, and George's face lights up with appreciation.

George clasps the pink microphone between her thighs, because she's using her hands to knot friendship bracelets. She already has a half dozen on her left wrist, in various rainbow shades. Her hair poufs out today, but she has the sides pulled back and twisted into a messy bun. I've never seen uglier jeans than the ripped-up acid wash pair she wears, but I doubt she'd care if I shared my opinion.

"So, I'm here because all my jobs started to run together in my head. I kept using the wrong names and mixing up plotlines, and I guess the Author who complained about me thought I needed a mental health check."

"And do you agree?" Angela prods.

"No. All the characters I play are essentially the same character. Pretty, quirky, profound, but with some fatal flaw keeping me from being too unrelatable to audiences. And the plots are the same too. I shake up some poor sod's life, and he goes on to grander things without me. It's depressing."

"So would you say you're depressed?" Angela seems concerned.

George stops knotting to consider this question. "Maybe? But maybe I'm just bored. What do I have to look forward to? An endless parade of derivative tripe. I pray for something original to come my way, but it never does. So I keep on keeping on, but the joy in my work is gone."

"Let's go to the group for suggestions," Angela suggests. "What are some ways the rest of you cope when you struggle to get through your days? Do you take a warm, relaxing soak in the tub? Do you seek solace in the beauty of nature? Or do you visit a trusted friend for a chat? All of these simple activities are ways we might engage in self-care."

"First of all," Nebraska offers sweetly, "it helps to not think of it in terms of struggle. Every day and every project gives us an opportunity to shine our brightest. Does life hand us lemons sometimes? Sure. No one understands that better than I do. But I plant that lemon and it grows into a beautiful tree."

"Of more lemons," George says dryly.

"You can think of it that way if you want to," Nebraska counters, "but I choose to see the whole tree."

"Well, I think you've muddled your metaphor."

"Ladies," Angela interjects. "Enough. What we're touching on here is the question of attitude. You can't control the actions of others, Authors in particular, but you can control your reactions. In that vein, I have an assignment for you— something to think about between sessions."

We all protest. Hatred of homework universally connects the human race.

Angela continues, undeterred. "I want each of you to be vigilant in tracking your emotional reactions to the actions of others. Recognize your reaction in the moment, and if it is negative, ask yourself how you can change your attitude towards a more positive one."

Thinking positively generally comes easily to Manic Pixies. Despite feeling nervous about the potential risk involved in pursuing Zelda, I'm not worried about Angela's assignment. George and Nebraska, however, may encounter some difficulty considering the way they are exchanging death glares.

"Thanks, Angela," George says with false cheer. "You've really put things in perspective for me, and I'm so blessed to be among friends. So much so I made you all a little something."

She begins to distribute her friendship bracelets. Red for Mandy, orange for Chloe, green for me, and blue for Sky. She gives a purple one to Angela, pausing to help Angela tie it on her wrist. "The yellow one is for Zelda and this black one is for me. Oops, I guess I didn't make enough, Nebraska. Sorry!"

"Uh . . . that's wonderful, George. Now who wants some pecan pie?" Angela asks, her cheeks flushed. "Doesn't it smell delicious?"

George and Nebraska are still staring each other down, but the rest of us jostle one another to be first in line. Chloe wins the honor of slicing the pie. Meanwhile, Angela leaves, seemingly extremely eager to flee the scene.

"I hope you realize," Nebraska says, glowering at George but addressing the group at large, "that instead of trying to sugarcoat everything in positivity, all of you need to be taking a harder look at yourselves."

"What do you mean?" George demands.

"As a Legacy, I have access to privileged information. And I happen to know you all are in therapy because you are hot messes and the Council is losing its patience with you."

"And you're just so perfect," George scoffs.

"I'm not here because I have to be." Nebraska flips the longer sections of her hair over her shoulder. "I'm here out of the goodness of my heart. To help you realize your potential."

"You're here to troll us," counters Sky, stepping over to stand shoulder-to-shoulder with George. "You've never been interested in befriending the rest of us. You just enjoy putting us down so you can feel better about yourself."

The tension is too much for my Manic Pixie programming to take. I hold up the pie. "C'mon, a pie this good deserves to be shared. We can feed the nuts to the Stock Squirrels in Seasons Park."

Mandy and Chloe exchange glances. "Field trip!"

"I'm not getting my hands all filthy for the benefit of Stock Squirrels," Nebraska says dismissively.

"Good," George retorts as the rest of us head for the door. "Because no one invited you."

CHAPTER 25

Needless to say, we make some Stock Squirrels in Seasons Park manically happy during our pecan distribution session. I'm more grateful than ever that we've so easily bonded as a group, Nebraska notwithstanding.

As soon as I arrive home, my Author summons button lights up. Instead of being bummed, I'm energized by the prospect of hanging out with Ava again. I'm sure it would please the TropeTown Council to know that. Maybe therapy can reform me after all.

Backstage, I guzzle down a half-gallon of tomato juice at the craft services table before I notice this pretentious prat smirking at me.

"Ah, Marsden! We finally meet!" He extends his hand, and my automatic reflex is to shake it—something I regret as soon as his iron grip squeezes the life out of my fingers.

"Sorry, you are?"

"Rafferty. Your rival for the affections of our dear Ava." He wrinkles his snooty nose. "And a far superior one."

I can't imagine what anyone, let alone Ava, sees in this guy. It can't be his fake British accent, or his tasseled penny loafers and plaid bow tie, or the contract he has clearly signed with

OPEC for the barrels of oil he needs to slick back his hair and shellac his beard.

"Where's Ava?"

"I imagine she's recuperating from our last scene, considering how . . . vigorous it became." He actually winks at me. Disgusting. "But the Author tells me this next chapter is just you and me, mate."

Since he's the spitting image of a Hipster Douche, imagine my shock to learn this tool is a Developed. As far as getting a Happily Ever After with Ava goes, this puts me at a distinct disadvantage, and this smarmy jerk knows it. What he doesn't know is I'm not putting my eggs in Ava's basket, so it's not like I care. But my point is, I don't have to let this dude's attitude ruin my mood. Again, I have therapy to thank for this insight.

"Sounds like a rollicking good time," I say blandly. I maintain an intense focus on the cheese spread and cracker display and ignore his repeated attempts to piss me off.

Finally, the Author calls us to do the scene.

The set-up goes like this: Rafferty has come to my house to pick up a sweater Ava left behind after our study session. A storm lurks on the horizon, both literally and metaphorically. This is called an objective correlative, in literary terms.

Rafferty knocks, seven times in rapid succession, something he copied from Ava once upon a time.

Expecting Ava, due to her signature knock, I bound to the door and fling it open. And stop dead in my tracks.

"Uh, who are you?"

"Ava's boyfriend." Rafferty flexes his puny biceps. "And you're the chap who will keep his distance from Ava from now on."

The Author types that I look hurt and betrayed, but instead of following directions, I bust up laughing at Rafferty's poor attempt to act tough. How am I supposed to take him seriously?

"Sorry!" I aim my apology upward toward the rafters—at the Author, not at Rafferty.

The Author strikes my reaction, her furious pounding of the delete key echoing through the soundstage.

We try again.

This time, I look hurt and betrayed. "Why are you here?"

"Just be a good lad and hand over Ava's sweater," Rafferty says. "Then I'll be on my way."

"Ava left it here on purpose. So I'll keep it unless she tells me otherwise."

We continue to exchange barbs for several pages, and I struggle to make sense of the narrative relevance of this encounter. In my opinion, it's longwinded and lacks any nuance. Not that it's my place to question the Author, as Angela would certainly remind me.

The more we argue, the less I can stand to be in the same room with this guy.

Unfortunately, the Author keeps at the scene for hours, cutting a word or two here, adding a phrase there, putting us through the paces over and over.

Rafferty remains unruffled.

Finally, we hear ripping followed by a whoosh, the telltale sounds of a scene being trashed.

"Bloody hell!" Rafferty exclaims, narrowing his eyes in my direction. "That was some of my best work."

I wish the Author would trash Rafferty.

CHAPTER 26

Yellow and black crime scene tape crisscrosses the doorframe of our group therapy room when I arrive in the morning. Gray smoke billows, and the stench of burnt plastic assaults my nose. All the other girls, with the exception of Nebraska, mill about farther down the hallway. Zelda waves, which lifts my spirits despite the wreckage. I peek into the room. Angela stands coughing amidst warped furniture and bubbled wallpaper. When she sees me, she extricates herself with a contorted shimmy between the tape and slams the door behind her.

"What happened?" I ask.

"The inspector suspects arson, but according to protocol, I can't elaborate on the details."

"Arson?" TropeTown doesn't experience much crime, at least not on the Right Side of the Tracks. A giant electric fence ensures the Tropes in the Villain Zone don't mingle or practice their devilish deeds on the rest of us.

"Most curious, isn't it?" Angela muses. "Someone from the Council will be here shortly to speak with us. She may tell us more."

I think back to Angela claiming our therapy room was a safe space. If the Council didn't see who set the fire, then they must not have video cameras in the therapy rooms.

I follow Angela down the hallway to where the others now sit in a semicircle on the floor. Mandy pulls some pink bottles full of bubbles out of her giant handbag. Angela watches morosely as we commence a bubble war. We aim for one another's heads, dissolving into laughter whenever a bubble pops directly between someone's eyes.

Our revelry is cut short by the Council member's arrival. This angular woman wears a powder-puff blue power suit, the kind with the boxy cut and huge shoulder pads. She clacks her heels across the floor until she towers over us. "No need to get up," she declares. But her tone is so icy that all of us immediately scramble into a standing position and hide the plastic wands behind our backs. Should I salute her or something?

"Hi Bridget," Angela says warmly. "Thank you for taking time out of your busy schedule to come by. Do we have a new room assignment yet?"

Angela's greeting does nothing to thaw Bridget's demeanor. "No need to worry about that."

Angela blinks in confusion. "Why not?"

"We in the Council appreciate your exemplary service with these . . . Manic Pixies," Bridget says, her words dripping with scorn. "I'm sure this particular Trope gave you quite the challenge."

Immediately catching on to Bridget's use of the past tense, Angela draws a sharp breath. "Are you firing me?"

Bridget laughs. "Why, no my dear. We are canceling this therapy group, effective immediately, but that's not a reflection on you. Please stop by the employment office at your earliest convenience for reassignment."

"What?" Chloe bursts out. "Why is therapy canceled?"

Bridget gives her a cold look. "It's become clear your type is . . . problematic. This latest incident has confirmed that our support resources will be put to better use elsewhere."

Problematic? What does that even mean? It seems strange that the Council would go to all the effort of sending us threatening letters about termination and setting us up in group therapy just to cancel it because our meeting place is a burnt-out husk.

"So what now?" Mandy asks. "We're just free to go on with our lives? What about all our problems that brought us here?"

"Yes, well, there are those famous words to live by: *Eat, drink, and be merry.*" Bridget smiles indulgently and pats Mandy on the head. The fact that these words are usually followed by *For tomorrow we must die* is ominous enough to give me pause.

Bridget swivels on her heel and marches toward the elevators. The doors open for her immediately and swallow her up.

For once, we are rendered speechless. I'm not sure how to sort through the implications of this. At the forefront of my brain, though, is the delightful notion that dating Zelda is no longer forbidden.

I turn my head to catch Zelda's eye, hoping she might give me one of her signature saucy winks, but I only catch sight of her fading out in the glow of an Author summons. She sure has been working a ton lately.

"I don't have a great feeling about this," Sky says. "I mean, not that I dig therapy or anything, but Bridget was just so . . . dismissive of us. She scares me."

I remember what Nebraska told us about the Council losing patience with us. At the time, it seemed like merely another trademark Nebraska insult, but what if there was more to it? It's not like me to be paranoid, but this whole scene has an unsettling undercurrent, and I have trouble wrapping my brain around it.

"I . . . I don't know what to tell you," Angela stammers. "But I'll . . . see what I can find out. Maybe once the Council gets to the bottom of who set this fire, they'll be willing to reinstate our therapy session . . ."

She trails off. Whereas my fellow Manic Pixies are simply confused, Angela seems as gutted as our former room. Clearly she's not used to having her sessions canceled so abruptly and with so little explanation. Her expression sends shockwaves of existential dread through my body.

"I think we should stick together no matter what," I say.

"Yes," Chloe says. "Maybe our official therapy is canceled, but that doesn't mean we can't meet up on our own somewhere."

Angela shakes herself out of her stupor and says with false cheer, "That's a wonderful idea. I'll be in touch as soon as I know more." She goes down the line of us—Mandy, Sky, Chloe, George, and me—giving us hugs like we're her baby chicks. She dabs at her cheeks with the hem of the long trumpet sleeves of her shirt. As she makes her way over to the elevator, swaying as she walks, the rest of us huddle up in solidarity.

"This isn't goodbye," Mandy says firmly. Trust Mandy to not know how to end something. To lighten the mood, she does a spontaneous handstand, almost hitting me in the face with one of her gladiator sandals.

A curious euphoric lightness takes over my body, and I burst out laughing. My hysteria soon infects the others.

Of course, it doesn't last. Whoever said laughter is the best medicine not only didn't fully appreciate the miracle of cough drops, but also didn't consider laughter doesn't cure you—it merely transfers the pain to your abs temporarily.

CHAPTER 27

I end up moping around most of the rest of the morning, too restless to nap but too depressed to play music or take a walk. I find that as much as I hated the idea of going to therapy, I already miss it. Sure, I have my work, but since I lost Finn, my time hanging around in TropeTown has lacked pizzazz. In just a few short sessions, therapy gave me a sense of belonging and a whole group of friends. But did we make a true, lasting connection? Or will we drift apart without this common obligation? We all have our separate projects, and none of us are programmed to be especially sentimental.

My mind naturally drifts to Zelda. Even though therapy meant I couldn't ask her out, at least I could look forward seeing her almost every day. Will I even have the chance to tell her how I feel about her now?

And I keep going back to the way Bridget acted. Her attitude was so full of contempt, not just for our group, but for the whole Manic Pixie Trope.

A pounding at the door saves me from my spiraling thoughts. I jump up eagerly, crossing my fingers it's Zelda. But when I answer, I uncross them. It's Angela.

"Good afternoon, Riley. Are you ready to go?"

For a second, I'm paralyzed with an irrational fear she's here to escort me to the Termination Train. But I force myself to smile and hope positivity will follow. "Uh, sure. Where are we going?"

"Nebraska's. She offered to host us from now on. Informally, of course. Everyone else is already there."

Despite the weight of all that's happened today, I can't suppress a glimmer of glee. One does not simply walk into Trope-Town Heights. Your name has to appear on the guest list at the golden gates. I have to admit, Nebraska's impromptu invitation makes me feel like a celebrity, even though I'm only going as part of an entourage.

"I'm ready."

There are so many things I want to ask Angela, but she has already turned away from me to flag down a bicycle taxi. When the driver stops for us, Angela runs her red admin card through his payment machine as we get in. We fit snugly due to her massive thigh muscles, which rival those of our driver. "TropeTown Heights," she says.

Our driver tips his denim cap at us and starts to pedal.

The world feels different from the back seat of a bicycle taxi. This guy pumps his legs like a professional racer, so scenery passes by us in a blur. Buildings run together. Pedestrians fade into the background. Even the birds in the sky can't keep up with our pace. Cool gusts of air whip at our hair, blowing it backward off our faces. And this same wind whistles through the spokes of the wheels, an insistent sound warning people to get out of our way.

Once I'm breathing normally again, I sneak a peek at Angela to gauge whether she's getting as much of a rush from this ride as I am, but it's hard to tell. Her eyes are closed and her mouth is slightly open. As always, her posture is inhumanly perfect, and her hands rest lightly on her knees. The prayer beads on her right wrist nestle against the purple friendship bracelet from George.

She seems much less upset than she was this morning, but of course, she's a professional therapist, so she's trained to set aside her own feelings and focus on her charges.

Though technically, we're not her responsibility any longer. The fact that she's here at all indicates that she's genuinely on our side.

I clear my throat. "Do you ride in these often?"

"Usually only for official TropeTown business," she states with a note of finality, indicating that this is all I can expect to weasel out of her.

But I'm curious about Angela now, and I want to know something real about her, something that can't be found on her character trait sheet. If you want to unlock someone's personal secrets, sometimes it helps to offer to share your own.

"This is my first time," I admit. "I've never ridden any form of transportation before."

"Not surprising." She's right, of course. Regular Tropes, especially new ones like me, don't usually get the chance to experience such luxury. But she doesn't need to sound so dismissive.

She seems to take note of my hurt expression because she softens her tone and says almost tenderly, "Work hard and someday you can be Legacy, too. And you can ride in these all the time. Like Nebraska." Her nose wrinkles when she says Nebraska's name.

"Oh, I am working hard," I assure her, changing tactics to give her a heaping helping of praise. "I've been following your advice from our sessions, and everyone at my current job seems to be happy with me. So thank you."

She smiles, and her shoulders relax a smidge. "That's wonderful to hear. And you're welcome." Even though I can tell she's trying to sound cheerful, I detect an undertone of sadness. Does she somehow think it's her fault the Council cancelled our therapy? Does she feel like she failed us? It seems too personal of a question to ask, so I ask something else.

"You must have a ton of experience. Did you start out doing Trope work in novels?"

"I did. I found being a part of stories incredibly fulfilling, but my Trope rarely gets to have much of a . . . social life. And the locations don't vary much. Office. Therapy room. Maybe an occasional house call."

Angela always insists on embracing our Tropes, so it's disconcerting to hear her disparage hers as so limiting. "So you switched over to being a Service Trope for more variety?"

"I fell in love with someone. And she encouraged me to take this position." She sighs. "I haven't regretted my career change, even if I sometimes rue the day I met that girl."

So even therapists have romantic troubles. Though I can technically date Zelda now, I don't really feel like confiding in Angela about my crush. Even so, it seems like she's capable of understanding the particular pain of uncertain romance. I wonder who broke her heart.

"Did she give you that?" I point at her ring.

Angela twists the ring on her thumb, as if just realizing that she's wearing it. "Yes. How'd you figure?"

"I don't know. Maybe a ring that's too big for your ring finger is a metaphor for a love that's too big to hold on to. Or something."

She snorts. "Or something. That's for sure. I got these prayer beads because of her."

"Sorry."

"Don't be. Every relationship teaches us something important about ourselves. Especially the tough ones."

"I prefer the easy ones." I laugh.

I expect her to laugh, too, but she doesn't. "You're an insightful young man, Riley. I believe you have the potential to go so far. But real personal growth is never easy. Trust your instincts and ignore the distractions."

I'm confused. This conversation seems to have gotten away from me. But our driver pulls up to TropeTown Heights' gates, and Angela hops out before I can ask for clarification.

She gives our names at the guard station. The golden gates open, and the splendor that greets me makes me forget all my questions.

CHAPTER 28

A bedazzled sign beyond the gates of TropeTown Heights promises us awe-inspiring opulence, and I can't disagree. As we strut along the yellow bricks of the main road, a light breeze caresses us with the intoxicating scent of rose petals. Each mansion exudes charm and beauty, with lavish details ranging from intricate latticework to imposing turrets.

One of the estates we pass features a hedge maze and a giant bay window through which I can see a movie-screen-sized portrait of a collie wearing a blue windbreaker and sunglasses, meaning the collie I met in the elevator my first day of therapy must be Legacy.

Angela encourages me to keep moving. "You can gape all you want on your way out."

She turns down a picturesque lane bordered by a low stone wall stained by verdigris. It must be an intentional flaw, because everything else in this part of town sparkles with perfection. Weeping willows bend their leaves toward us on the path down the lane, blocking our view of Nebraska's residence until we arrive at her wraparound porch.

Other than the lavender exterior, the house could pass for a southern plantation home with its stately columns and row of upstairs galleries over the porch. White wooden shutters frame the open French windows, and piano music drifts lazily from somewhere inside.

Angela presses the doorbell, Nebraska's one acquiescence to modernity. Chimes go off and seconds later, the door sweeps open to reveal the mistress of the house.

"Welcome!" Nebraska ushers us into her foyer, but all my attention goes to the winding staircase behind her and the dome above her. She leads us back through her giant ballroom—a space featuring cherry hardwood and the blue crystal chandelier that Mandy mentioned that day in the cafeteria—and onto her veranda where all the girls sit at a rectangular dining table. I'm ecstatic to be in their company again. Alas, Zelda sits hunched over a notebook, writing, and doesn't look up.

The table is set with delicate, painted teacups on saucers over lace, and a three-tiered pumpkin pie forms the centerpiece.

"I'll be right back." Nebraska picks up a pitcher and a coffee carafe. "With fresh beverages."

Mandy pats the empty seat next to her. "Riley, this place setting has your name all over it."

And it does. On ivory cardstock. Written in calligraphy.

Nebraska has put herself at the head of the table, next to me. Angela is at the opposite end.

While Zelda continues to scrawl and ignore me, and the other girls chat amongst themselves, Mandy leans in toward me.

"You missed all the drama," she says in a low, breathy voice. But even when she's clearly ready to gossip, she still comes off as innocuous as a fawn. It's gotta be those eyes and those red, red lips.

"That's okay, I'm sure there's more to come." I'm actually

kind of amazed that the girls look so relaxed after this morning's upheaval. It's natural for Manic Pixies to recover their equilibrium quickly, but I'm still shaken from the arson and the encounter with Bridget. It seems that I'm straying from my programming. Am I developing complexity, or do I simply have a glitch?

"So, Nebraska threw this all together by herself," Mandy says.

I'm impressed. Nebraska has some serious hasty hostess skills.

"But she complained about how the Council outlawed live-in staff because they now consider those Tropes degrading. Apparently she prefers the good ole days."

Nebraska glides in with her refreshed beverages. She places the pitcher in front of Angela. She takes her place and sets the carafe in front of me. She pushes creamer my way. "Soy milk."

Again, I'm impressed.

Angela clears her throat, loudly, and the conversation dies down. "We've all had quite a shock today. I'm sorry to report that I don't have any additional information regarding the abrupt cancellation of your official therapy yet, but I'm committed to seeing you survive and thrive. While I'm no longer your therapist, I am happy to serve in a mentor capacity at your gatherings, if you'll have me?"

None of us hesitates to affirm this. I'm touched that she cares enough about us to continue to work with us. And I regret ever thinking anything unkind about her.

"Also," Angela continues, "I'd like to thank Nebraska for inviting us to meet here."

"Oh, it's my pleasure," Nebraska gushes. "I do so enjoy entertaining my dear friends."

George rolls her eyes at this. "Speaking of friends, my friendship bracelet has gone missing."

I glance around the circle and notice everyone wears the bracelets George gave us. Does Nebraska have something to do with the mysterious disappearance of George's bracelet? Judging from the expressions on everyone else's faces, I am not alone in this line of thinking. No one accuses her of anything, though, not even George.

"Oh Georgina! You're so delightfully scatterbrained!" Nebraska giggles. She stirs creamer into her coffee with a fork.

"How many times do I have to tell you not to call me that?" If faces were flamethrowers, George's would be shooting fire right now.

Angela puts up her hand. "Girls! Let's show one another respect. Okay? In my capacity as your mentor, I will still rely on my therapy background and methods, but I also want you to feel comfortable with me. If George wants us to call her George, then let's call her George. Can you manage that, Nebraska?"

Nebraska's eyes flash, but she nods curtly.

"Excellent. Now, I think it would be good for us all to continue in the same vein as before—sharing what led us to be in this group in the first place. And based on our schedule, Mandy is up today."

Mandy folds her hands into the lap of her incredibly puffy white skirt. "But what's the point of talking through our issues if the Council thinks we're too much hassle?"

"Yeah," I chime in, because this strikes the worried chord inside me. "What's going to happen to us now that we seem to be on the Council's bad side?"

"The Council's primary concern is investigating the fire," Angela says carefully. "Your primary concern is to figure out what has been holding you back from being your best selves. So let's focus on you."

I can hardly believe that a few days ago, I thought Angela was merely a tool of the Council. Whatever else is going on here, it seems clear now she's committed to our improvement project.

She gestures at Mandy, who takes a sip of her water, dabs her lips, and says, "I'm here because I got too distracted by the drama in my personal life. You all know about this thing I have with Clark." Mandy stares at her knees while she talks. "It's like a bumper car ride I can't seem to drive away from."

"How many times have you broken up with him now?" Zelda asks. It's so considerate of her to finally put away her notebook and acknowledge that the rest of us exist.

I sound bitter, don't I? I am not used to unrequited crushes and the particular anguish that accompanies them. In my Novels, even when I have romantic rivals, I've always been cast as the heartbreaker, not the heartbroken.

Mandy bites her red lip. "Ummm . . . this is going to sound awful, but I've lost count. Maybe twenty-two times?"

"Dang, girl!" I pat her arm protectively. I knew Mandy and Clark have differing opinions on the usefulness of blown glass, but I had no idea their relationship has been this fraught.

"Why do you think you have trouble letting go of him?" Angela asks.

Meanwhile, Nebraska kicks up her legs over the side of the armrest and lies back in a swoon. Angela ignores her, so we do, too.

Mandy picks at her teal polish, chipping it off her pinkie nail in tiny chunks. "He's so enthusiastic about me. I guess he makes me feel worth being enthusiastic about."

"Your value is never in question," Angela says with surprising force, like she takes it personally. "It doesn't change based on whether other people appreciate you."

Mandy shrinks into herself. "I wish I could believe that," she whispers, so quietly I'm probably the only one who can hear her. She continues more audibly, "It always goes in a pattern. First, he smothers me. I feel like I can't breathe, and I break up with him. For a few days, I'm full of resolve that I'm better off without him. And then, I get restless and lonely and unsure. He comes around and reminds me how awesome I am, and I take him back."

"You *are* awesome!" Chloe high-fives her from her other side.

Zelda jumps out of her chair. "Yeah you are!" She rounds the table and pulls Mandy up for a hug.

"Group hug!" Sky squeals, and we all pile on until we spin like a carousel of celebration. George's arm flails out and knocks over a teacup, which shatters on the marble floor. Angela regards us from her chair with a raised eyebrow.

Nebraska falls to pieces over her broken teacup. "It's vintage!" she fumes. She turns on George with a clenched fist. "You did that on purpose."

George backs away. "I didn't!"

I tense as they face off. They've been revving for a full-on fight, and Nebraska looks ready to rumble.

"Everyone sit down," Angela barks, and we scramble to obey like chastised puppies.

Nebraska unclenches her fist and snaps her fingers. Her purple tones of rage disappear, and she smiles sunny yellow. "It's okay. People are always more important than things."

Because her delivery comes out a tad too flat, I'm not convinced she actually means it.

"Well stated," Angela says. "As a person, you have intrinsic significance. And while I like that you all are so supportive of each other, Mandy needs to stop relying on external validation—even that given by friends—and start practicing internal validation. Mandy—you said Clark reminds you how awesome you are, but why can't you remind yourself?"

"I guess I can try." Mandy's pained expression reveals that she has her doubts.

"Why don't we all try?" Angela pounds her palm on the table and the china clatters. "Repeat after me: I am awesome."

As usual in forced public mantra repetitions, most of us mumble. It's not that I don't think I'm awesome, but isn't it a mite vain to scream it at the top of my lungs? Nebraska has no such qualms. Her clear voice soars with confidence.

Angela shakes her head. "Is that the best you can do?"

"I am awesome," we say. Louder now, but still reluctant.

"No pie until I'm satisfied with your awesomeness," Angela threatens, hitting me right where it does the most damage.

"I am awesome!" And this time the blue chandelier in the ballroom quivers before the boom in my voice.

CHAPTER 29

Immediately after our session, while I'm preoccupied with pie, Zelda scrams. Which puts a damper on my plans to walk around admiring TropeTown Heights with her, so I gawk at all the ostentation by myself until I get hungry enough to go home for lunch.

I've just settled into my sofa when there's a scraping at my door again. I expect to see Sprite, but Zelda stands there instead.

"Sprite told me scratching gets your attention." Zelda imitates a paw with her hand.

I survey the area around my stoop, but no Sprite. I raise an eyebrow. "She talks, does she?"

"To kindred spirits she does!"

Honestly, I am prone to believe anything Zelda tells me, plausible or not. "So you're the cat whisperer now. Sure, okay."

"Aren't you going to invite me in? I brought you a gift."

"Gift first," I joke. "And if I approve, I will consider your request for admittance."

She holds out a silver button, this one with Au-79, the symbol for gold. "I left in such a rush because I wanted to make you something. It's to help you remind yourself how awesome you are. But since there's no AW . . ."

"I'm glad you went with that rather than As-33."

She laughs approvingly. "Yes. Arsenic would send a very different kind of message, wouldn't it?"

"It's why I never eat powered doughnuts."

"Same here!"

It may be a small similarity, but I latch onto it as proof of our compatibility.

"In that case, you may pin me and then enter." I bow formally.

She steps close in order to affix the pin to my collar. Kissing distance. I hold my breath until she finishes with a graze of her knuckles against my chin. Accidental? On purpose? My racing heartbeat would like to believe the latter.

But as soon as she sets foot on the rug in my living room, she quirks an eyebrow. It makes me super nervous that my apartment doesn't live up to her standards and she'll never want to return.

"May I offer you a spot of tea?" I attempt to mask the shakes in my voice with a phony British accent that would make Rafferty proud. "I have Double O Cinnamon." *Which I bought in case you ever visited.*

"I'd love some, thank you."

When I return with two steaming mugs of tea, she's flipping through the comic book I was in the middle of when she showed up.

"I love Maya's art. She has such a bold vision for the reboot of these characters."

Does Zelda need to know I wasn't aware that an earlier version exists? Nope. "Totally."

"Aha! Gotcha!" She points her trigger finger at me. "You don't know a thing about comics, do you?"

Oh no. "How could you tell?"

"While checking out your bookshelf, I discovered a curious anomaly. You have a bunch of random issues of different books."

She stands and pulls out a couple of examples. "Look here. You have Razzle-Dazzle Spider-Mouse 89 and Jazz-Hands Spider-Mouse 90. Did these even make sense when you read them? They're two different universes with two different continuities! And another thing: you don't protect your books—you stuff them in between atlases and dictionaries all willy-nilly."

Undone by a rookie mistake. Ah, geekdom—you are a cruel mistress.

"Riley, comics demand zealous engagement. A sincere fan stocks up on boards and bags and boxes, and debates endlessly about the obvious superiority of his or her preferred universe. Tell me, are you willing to make such a serious commitment?"

Her impassioned speech transforms my shame into conviction. "I am."

"Then we gladly welcome you to the fold."

"You do?"

"Yeah, I'll take you by the comic store in the mall sometime if you want."

I'd go to a clown convention if it meant getting to hang out with Zelda. "Sign me up."

She blows on her tea and takes an exploratory sip. "Ahhh. Perfect drinking temperature."

I clink my mug against hers and drink too. The tea tastes spicy and silky on my tongue. "Good stuff."

"Looks like we both have a license to chill," she says with a wink.

I'm flattered she repeats my joke despite disparaging it last time. It feels like progress.

We sip the tea and keep catching each other's eye. I work up the courage to bring up what's really on my mind. "So, we're not officially in therapy together anymore . . ." I trail off hoping she catches my drift.

"It's so great of Angela not to give up on us," Zelda says, possibly ignoring my drift. "I was suspicious of her at first, but now I really do feel like she's on our side. Don't you?"

I am so not thinking about Angela right now. But I do notice Zelda is clutching her tea mug like it might run off to the Villain Zone, and I remember what Mandy said about Zelda having different priorities. Maybe I'll chase her away if I'm too direct. Maybe it would be a big mistake to try to define what we are to each other. Maybe I should just go with the flow and see what happens. "We're lucky to have her."

Zelda beams at me like I gave the correct answer and finishes off her tea. She sets her mug down and gets up to poke around my stuff again.

"Ooh, you play the guitar?" She picks it up and hands it to me.

I strum my go-to chords and improvise some silly lyrics. "I know a girl named Zelda. She wants to be a welder . . ."

"I do not!" she exclaims, laughing. "And that doesn't even rhyme."

I keep singing, undeterred by her near-valid criticism. "Transition metals won't sting her with nettles. And behold! The fates have foretold! You'll never grow mold when you join silver and gold."

She claps. She joins in with her own verse, singing adorably off-key. "I know a boy named Riley. He plays guitar so spryly. He's kind of a dork, should be stabbed with a spork . . ."

"Hey!" I protest, laughing.

She grins. "Genius inspires genius."

The more time I spend with her, the more she makes me fall for her. And now she's adding flattery into the mix. Be still my Pixie heart.

Pretty much every romantic comedy worth its blubbery feels features a montage sequence where the happy couple frolics and cavorts backed by an up-tempo pop song.

So I turn the radio way up to set the montage mood.

Zelda and I play darts, all the while laughing and touching and generally being cute. As I am sure you'd expect by now, she beats me.

We spin the globe and point out all the places we'd go if we lived in Reader World. Paris. Paramaribo. Pittsburgh.

We bounce around the kitchen chopping up pineapple, pitting cherries, and peeling bananas. We throw them all in a blender to make smoothies and race to see who can finish first. As I am sure you'd expect by now, I beat her.

I walk her halfway home (her idea, not mine), and she gives me one of those glorious full body hugs that's so cozy and perfect you could fall asleep standing up if you weren't mega turned on and concentrating on being thankful for the restrictive denim of your jeans.

Of course, I haven't forgotten we aren't actually a couple. But after today, I can feel the pulse of possibility. It's intoxicating.

And . . . fade out . . .

CHAPTER 30

The next day at Nebraska's mansion, Angela charges us with silent meditation and reflection about our awesomeness. So I meditate on Zelda's radiance and reflect on our afternoon spent being awesome together.

Zelda and Chloe both get Author summons near the end of our hour, and Angela leaves promptly when Nebraska's antique wood grandfather clock chimes ten. The others trickle out after her, but I stay and offer to help Nebraska clean up the mess.

"Have another piece of pie," she says by way of dastardly distraction. And of course it works. I do love my pie.

I'm cramming a third piece into my piehole when I get the urge to pee. Bad. I mentally revisit the four cups of coffee I drank—curse that sweet soy milk temptress!

"Uh . . . do you mind pointing the way to your bathroom?"

Nebraska opens the smaller door to the kitchen and gestures for me to pass. "Down the hall on your right."

I thank her and start my trek. The kitchen is gorgeous, full of chrome, teak, and rose marble. But my full bladder and I don't linger to admire the view.

The hallway goes on forever. When I open the doors I find:

1. A small room with wall-to-wall mirrors and four blue yoga mats on the floor
2. A room with wrapping paper and ribbons
3. A room full of plush velvet hatboxes in assorted colors with what look like handwritten letters spilling from them
4. A room that is completely empty except for a giant stuffed hippo wearing a diamond tiara
5. THE BATHROOM!

After I take care of my pressing need to recycle my coffee, I head back toward the veranda, but a nagging memory encourages me to make an unscheduled stop in the hatbox room. Didn't Nebraska say Finn wrote her letters? I mean, she also said she destroyed them, but my gut tells me to not trust her on this. If I find a letter from Finn, maybe it will shed some light on the secrets he took with him to the Termination Train.

The first few hatboxes contain fan mail, some of it dated decades ago with faded ink. Envy and self-doubt make me think I'm actually not that awesome, because I've only gotten a tiny fraction of Nebraska's audience adoration. I remind myself she's been at this way longer than I have. And also, I don't need external validation to be awesome.

"I am awesome!" I whisper-scream to myself. I can't be more vocally expressive because I don't want Nebraska to discover me rooting through her prized possessions. Which means I should also leave before she gets suspicious that I'm taking too long.

I open a hatbox decorated with hearts, hoping to see Finn's name, but instead I see Angela's name signed in bold cursive. What the heck? The box teems with letters from Angela. One envelope contains a photo of them with huge smiles and cheeks touching. All of the clues click into place. Oh. My. God. Why didn't I see it before? Angela and Nebraska used to be a couple.

Their animosity makes so much more sense now. Is Nebraska only attending therapy to piss off Angela? That would be vindictive of her, but it fits her modus operandi.

I quickly scan the rest of the open hatboxes. Nebraska calls my name in the same second that I finally spy Finn's handwriting on an envelope on a high shelf. But I don't have time to do anything but dash out of the room and hope she doesn't catch me snooping.

"Coming!" I shout down toward the kitchen.

She emerges into the hallway, her face creepy in the shadows thanks to the backlighting. "Hey," she says, her tone neutral. "I thought you might have gone for a swim in the sewer. Down with the crocs."

Does she suspect something? Maybe she's plotting to offer me up as a tasty overly caffeinated treat to her roving pack of sewer reptiles.

"Maybe next time." I laugh to cover up my paranoia. "I didn't bring my swim trunks." Next time I'll definitely find an excuse to return to the hatbox room and swipe that letter from Finn. If she lied about destroying it, it must contain something important.

As soon as I'm close enough, she hooks her arm through mine and leads me back to the veranda.

"I packed the leftover pie for you." She loads me up with a red felt pie box embossed with the name of a fancy Trope-Town Heights bakery. "Can't have it lying around here trying to seduce me."

"Riley saves the day!"

She pats the top of the box. "If you say so."

CHAPTER 31

Ava greets me with a kiss when I arrive backstage at work, which takes me by surprise. "I've decided I like kissing you better than Rafferty."

I can't deny her announcement massages my ego most ergonomically, and in my head I shout, "I am awesome!" and "Suck it, Rafferty!" But now that Zelda and I are *maybe* fast-tracking it to coupledom, I probably shouldn't be letting Ava give me sugar behind the scenes.

The Extras grazing at the craft services table seem supportive, though, judging by their clapping and cheering.

"Nice to see you, too." I squeeze her hand, but also step back. "So what's on the docket for today?"

"We're waiting for TropeTown to send over a dog to play Bruiser, and then we'll take a walk with him in the park."

Considering our wardrobe—T-shirts and sweatpants—I predict running and possible canine shenanigans.

"So this will be your first encounter with Bruiser?"

"First time meeting a dog ever!" She bounces up and down on the balls of her feet.

"Really?" It strikes me how limited Ava's experience will always be. While as a Developed she has the privilege of touching Readers' lives, she'll be eternally stuck in a world only as large as what the Author gives her. As a Trope, I may not stick in Readers' minds for long, but I've been given the potential for a much wider range of adventures. Of course, I'm greedy and I want more. Isn't there a way to have it all?

"Oh, look! There he is!"

I glance over at the landing area and recognize a familiar blue windbreaker and sunglasses.

After the brown and white collie laps up an entire bowl of water, he trots over to us. "Hey—you're the kid we mistook for a New Age Therapist. How's therapy been treating you?"

Ava's eyes widen in horror. Leave to a dog to let the cat out of the bag.

"Just fine, Bruiser," I say through clenched teeth. I guess he hasn't heard about our therapy being canceled, and I don't exactly want to discuss that right now. "How's yours?"

"Call me Sal."

I cross my arms. "I wouldn't expect a Legacy like yourself would go for such a minor role."

"It's essentially a cameo. A couple of days' work at most. Good visibility in a projected blockbuster. Plus, I'm tired of doing death scenes."

Ava kneels in front of him. "Is it okay if I scratch behind your ears? Dogs like that, right?"

"Starting out on the right paw," Sal says.

While Ava acquaints herself with Sal, I change into my wardrobe. The pants the Author chose fit me in terms of size, but not personality, unless she means for me to wear the repetitive print of the high school's snarling wolf mascot ironically. The plain but tight sweatshirt accentuates my chest, so I can hardly complain about that.

The green light beckons everyone to the stage, including the Extras. On the way, Bruiser shrugs out of his windbreaker and sunglasses, so he can act like a Reader World dog. Ava puts a collar on him and attaches a retracting leash.

The Author sketches the barest outline of a park. Trees, grass, running paths, and benches. The Extras mill around aimlessly while Ava and I stay on a dirt running path with Bruiser.

We run, Bruiser barking along beside us.

Nothing else happens for a while. The three of us wait for the Author to give us more to do. I imagine her staring at her screen, pondering what obstacles to throw in our way next to create tension and force us to overcome our challenges. Perhaps she sits at a desk, rereading coffee-stained notes to herself and toggling between her word processing tab and her social media accounts.

Ava doesn't seem to be bothered by this state of perpetual delay. She sports the blissful smile and heavy eyelids of someone with a runner's high.

I, however, develop a leg cramp.

The stage door opens and a new player, and another familiar face, joins our scene: the Stock Squirrel, in the process of removing his plaid bowtie.

I raise my hand to wave at the same time that the Author's fingers begin to fly across her keys. This results in Bruiser gunning for the Stock Squirrel and yanking his leash right out of Ava's grasp.

"Bruiser!" Ava shouts. "Bad dog!"

Ava and I finally catch up to him, but he wriggles away and puts us through a series of antics to rival the labors of Hercules, including:

1. Mucking about in the mud and then shaking it off on us
2. Chewing on the wheel of a stroller for which we receive a stern reprimand from a disgruntled mother
3. Ingesting a bar of chocolate someone dropped under a bench

Up until this last stunt, Ava and I laugh and forge a bond as a result of our trials. Bruiser finally allows Ava to catch him. She buries her face in his furry neck despite all the grime he acquired during his escapades.

"Dogs can't eat chocolate, or they'll die," she chokes out. "I have to get him to the vet."

I bend down and put my arm around her to comfort her. "I'll take you. He'll be fine."

Ava shakes out of my embrace. Vehemently. "No. I'll take him myself. This is all your fault, Marsden. If you weren't so distracting, he never could have gotten away from me."

"How was I distracting you?" I sputter.

"Don't try to charm your way out of this." She tugs on Bruiser's leash. "You know what you did."

"I really don't," I protest, but to no avail. Ava leaves the park without me, and as I watch her go, the clouds move to block out the sun.

Silence fills the soundstage and the green light blinks out.

CHAPTER 32

Ava and I head to Wardrobe to change out of our filthy costumes. She turns her back to me as she wrestles to lift her shirt over her head, so I turn around too, giving us both some privacy. The Burly Stagehand who ventures over to remove our cast-offs, on the other hand, cares not for our states of undress and taps his foot while waiting for us to finish.

When we're both dressed in our street clothes, Ava hugs me. "Hard day, right?"

"I have to wonder . . . why the unreasonable behavior toward Marsden?"

"I think I have some insight."

"Care to share?"

"Well, Rafferty works at the vet's office."

"So, you don't want him to see you and Marsden together." It comes out more accusatory than I intended.

Ava juts out her chin. "Hey, I'm not the writer. Don't blame me."

"You're right. I'm sorry."

"Don't mean to interrupt," Sal says. He needs a bath, but that hasn't stopped him from donning his blue windbreaker and sunglasses again. "Great working with you, kid. Hope to see you in the vet scene, though by the sounds of it, I probably won't. Hehe."

"Yeah, see you when I see you." He's irritated me enough that I don't mind his swift departure.

After Sal is gone, Ava leads me over to the row of chairs and sits me down. She looks so serious it's starting to freak me out. But she kneads my back with her knuckles, and I relax.

It feels so nice I close my eyes.

"Hey, Riley?" she says, her voice low and throaty and near.

"Mm-hmm."

"Why are you in therapy?"

My eyes fly open. I didn't expect that question right now, though I guess I should have. Darn that dog. "Ummm . . ."

"You don't have to tell me."

I turn to face her and take her hands in mine. A few days ago, I wouldn't have cared about Ava's opinion of me being in therapy, but there is this slowly growing achy spot in the middle of my heart that wants her to recognize and accept the real me. "You know novels don't always go as smoothly as Authors want them to. And sometimes the blame gets shifted to us Tropes. The TropeTown Council welcomes feedback from Authors about us, and sometimes that feedback criticizes our level of cooperation or adherence to the accepted qualities of our Trope."

She squeezes my fingers in solidarity. "That doesn't sound fair."

"When the Council received a second letter of complaint from an Author, I was assigned to group therapy, with a bunch of Manic Pixie Dream Girls."

"Girls?" She says it all high and squeaky and pulls away.

"Well, yeah. There aren't many boys in my Trope. In fact, I'm currently the only one."

"Are they pretty?" She looks at her fingernails, and I know I'm supposed to say no, but I'm sort of surprised she's jealous all of a sudden after teasing me so much with Rafferty.

"Of course." I keep my tone matter-of-fact. "By design. I mean, they are called 'dream girls,' which implies a certain level of attractiveness. You do know how Tropes work, don't you?"

"Yeah. They show us a video at orientation." She does this big dramatic sigh. "Do you find one of them particularly pretty?"

"Myself," I joke immediately, attempting to distract her from further inquiry.

She slaps my leg. "Ha ha. But seriously, like, is there someone you want to date in TropeTown?"

I squirm in the plastic chair, and the rivets on my back pockets scratch up against it unpleasantly. I debate whether I should tell her about Zelda.

The argument against telling her:

1. If Ava thinks she's the only girl in my life, our scenes will probably go more smoothly
2. It sucks to hear from someone you're into that they are into someone else
3. My relationship status with Zelda is murky and possibly forbidden, so the fewer people who know, the better

The argument for telling her:

1. It's unfair to Ava if I allow her to develop unrealistic expectations for our relationship—because this is

just a job for me and it's not like I'll be around forever even if the Author does go for #teammarsden

2. I respect Ava and I respect Zelda and I want to be honorable in my dealings with both of them

Can I just skip to the eating pie part of this scene now?

Coming up with my pros and cons takes such an unreasonably long time that Ava finally stands up with a fake, shiny happy expression. "You know what? Forget I asked. It doesn't matter."

She tromps off to the private entrance for Developeds. I should say something to make her feel better—or at least make an attempt to explain myself.

But I don't.

CHAPTER 33

After a restless night, I arrive at the TropeTown Heights guard station early. With the swagger of someone important, I give the Surly Security Guard my name.

"Sorry, fellow. Not on the list."

My swagger starts to sway. "Can you please check again? Nebraska expects me!"

"Oh, you're here for Nebraska. You're one of those *Manic Pixies*." He says this like we're all a bunch of rancid meat sticks. "Go on, then."

Relieved he's letting me though, I rush by him in case he changes his mind. Once out of his sight, though, I take time to smell the daffodils growing wild along the side of the golden brick road. What do daffodils smell like, you ask? Sort of sweet, but not cloying. And they symbolize new beginnings. I pick a bunch to put in a bouquet for Nebraska.

When I arrive, I skip the doorbell and walk around the side of the house to the veranda. Everyone occupies their same assigned seats, and Zelda scribbles in her notebook again, but at least she looks up this time and gives me a wink and a wave.

"Why how thoughtful, Riley!" Nebraska takes my daffodil offering and scuttles into the kitchen to find a vase.

George has a new craft today. She painstakingly sews buttons of all different shapes, sizes, and colors onto a cross-body sash. She wears one of her finished examples, and that together with her pigtail hairstyle makes her look super young, even though she's probably nearly as old as Nebraska.

Once Nebraska returns and sets the flower arrangement in the middle of the table next to today's delectable pie, Angela suggests we do trust exercises. I notice she has a wicked spark in her eye when she assigns George and Nebraska as partners.

George slams down her sash-in-progress, and buttons scatter.

"Oh, Georgina." Nebraska sounds like buttercream frosting on a day-old cupcake. "You don't have to worry I'll drop you. I'm the most trustworthy girl in our Trope."

"Don't call her that," Angela interjects, saving George from having to say what, by now, should be her trademarked catchphrase.

"Of course you are the *most* trustworthy." George glares. "You have to proclaim you're the best at everything."

Nebraska giggles sharply. "Why, my dear, that's because I am."

"Less talk and more action," Angela admonishes. "Let's go out to the lawn for this."

We all venture out onto Nebraska's bright green lawn, which is so lush I want to lie down and feel the fat blades of grass against my skin. We form a loose circle around Nebraska and George, who eye each other as if prepping for a cage fight instead of a trust exercise.

"Okay," Angela says. "So, Nebraska, you stand behind George, and you catch her."

"I understand what you mean for us to do . . ." Nebraska fastens the hooks and eyes on her corset top over her tank. "But what I don't understand is why you think thin little ole me could handle someone with such generous . . . curves."

The jab is classic Nebraska—complimentary if taken at face value, but clearly meant to wound.

George just laughs. She's proud of her hourglass figure, and she should be. "You *wish* you had my cup size."

"Please," Angela scoffs at Nebraska. "Like you don't spend hours sculpting your arms. You got this."

"Fine," Nebraska says. "But don't blame me if things go awry."

George gets into position and tips herself backwards. Nebraska catches her, but when she does, George cries out. "For fox sake!"

Angela hurries over to George's side. "What happened?"

"Nebraska pinched me!"

Nebraska puts on her best innocent expression. "I would never!"

That earns her an arched eyebrow from Zelda and eye-rolls from the rest of us.

George rubs the back of her neck, presumably the scene of the crime, and Angela inspects it. She runs her hands over George's skin.

"It is a bit red," Angela says. "But nothing conclusive."

George turns on Nebraska. "You've been out to get me since I started therapy."

"I'd be careful about making accusations about a Legacy," Nebraska says, keeping her tone friendly, despite the implied threat. "The Council wouldn't like it if they found out."

"Hrummph," George snorts, but she shuts up. She dutifully catches Nebraska without drama, and the big showdown fizzles out.

Chloe and Mandy go next, and Chloe ends up ripping the strap of Mandy's peach camisole while breaking her fall. George repairs the tear, patching it up with a constellation of purple buttons.

And now Angela assigns Zelda and me together, which makes me break into a mental happy dance.

Zelda stands a couple of feet in front of me and turns. She blows me a kiss over her shoulder, flustering me and making the other girls giggle. She's wearing a racer-back crushed velvet vest that exposes her sexy shoulder blades, and thanks to Angela, I have an excuse to touch them when she lands in my waiting arms.

"Thank you for being so trustworthy," she says when I help her back to her feet. "Your turn."

Maybe it's everyone staring at me with knowing smirks, but performance anxiety creeps up my spine, and I have to take several deep breaths to rein it in. What's the worst that can happen?

I spin around with my arms out like an airplane and hum to loosen up the atmosphere. Before my nerve flees for the hills, I flop backwards.

My upper back hits something soft and Zelda makes an oomph sound. We both lie on the springy, plush grass, with my head in Zelda's lap. It's both delightful and downright embarrassing, for a variety of reasons.

"Sorry!" I jump to my feet and swoop her up like I'm some kind of superhero. I settle her into her chair. "Are you okay?"

"I'm fine. But I failed to catch you." She massages her hip. "So don't apologize."

Our audience gives us some space. We all watch Angela and Sky run through the task effortlessly.

"Guess we're the biggest screw-ups out of all the screw-ups," Zelda remarks to me.

"Yes! We're the best at being the worst!" I give her a high five.

"That's one way to put it."

"Bravo!" Bridget approaches, struggling a bit in her heels on Nebraska's lawn while doing this super fake, sarcastic clapping motion. Angela stands stock still, like someone who has been caught committing a crime.

"Did I not disband your therapy with these Manic Pixies, Angela?" Bridget sneers. "No matter. I came to talk to Nebraska, but this pertains to all of you I suppose."

"May I offer you something to drink, Bridget?" Nebraska immediately jumps to perfect smarmy hostess mode. The rest of us are too scared of Bridget to say anything. We could be lawn statues—that's how silent and immobile we are.

"No thank you. I won't be here long." Bridget puts her hands on her hips. "Periodically the Council considers certain troublesome Tropes for retirement. You may not be familiar with the process, as it occurs relatively rarely. It is similar to termination, except instead of being levied on an individual basis, it applies to all members of a Trope. I regret to inform you that the Manic Pixie Trope is currently on our agenda."

The Manic Pixie contingent of lawn statues gasps.

"But why would you do that?" Sky demands. "It's not fair to punish our whole Trope because of one arson!"

I totally agree. Threatening us with full-scale extinction is an extreme reaction to a relatively small and contained fire. There has to be something more to this.

Bridget narrows her eyes at us, as if we're being overdramatic. "There are larger factors in play, I assure you. And I would encourage you not to think of it as a punishment. Should you be confirmed for retirement, each of you will have your consciousness preserved in the TropeTown archives, and you will be memorialized in the Trope Museum. These are privileges not awarded to characters who are terminated individually."

Knowing we'll be reduced to slides in a semi-forgotten archive in the Villain Zone is far from comforting. What did we ever do to deserve such a fate? Bridget is trying to spin it as some sort of honor, but being distilled down to my defining characteristics doesn't sound much better than being outright terminated.

"Since it would appear Angela has decided to voluntarily associate with you, perhaps she can help you come to terms with your . . . situation."

"Wait!" Nebraska finds her most indignant voice. "The Council cannot make a retirement determination until after holding a public meeting led by the Legacy members of the Trope."

Our heads all swivel toward Nebraska—our Trope's only Legacy. Our destiny is going to be in *her* hands?

Bridget nods briskly. "Indeed. It's our duty to give our Legacy members five days' notice before our final deliberations. These will take place at Town Hall at six p.m. this Wednesday. I look forward to hearing you plead your case then, Nebraska."

Bridget strides off, leaving a massive existential crisis in her wake.

CHAPTER 34

Memento mori is the Latin for "remember you must die." Mortality is not something a Manic Pixie spends eons contemplating, but I have faced up to its inevitability on occasion. For example, when I worked on the novel as the Manic Pixie Cancer Boy, I had scenes focused on living out your remaining time to the fullest. The inspiring underlying message is that every moment is a gift rather than a guarantee, so seize the day. I'll be the first to admit such axioms can seem overly trite. But when you are the one facing down the barrel of the gun, they become your lifelines.

If we only have five days to avert our Trope's full-scale demise, we're going to have to seize each of those days pretty intensely.

Our first order of business has to be gaining a voice at this Council meeting. No way can we leave our Trope's defense solely to Nebraska.

"You shouldn't have to be the only voice representing the whole Trope," I say to her in my best buttery baritone. "It's not fair to put such a huge burden on you."

"Yeah, even the *best* among us can use backup." Zelda catches my drift this time and layers on the kind of flattery

Nebraska can't resist. "What if we all make a presentation to the Council *together*? There's strength in numbers."

Nebraska looks at us thoughtfully. "So what are you suggesting?"

For this to work, Nebraska has to think our plan is her idea. "I don't know," I say. "You're the one with the most experience. We're all just offering to help out."

"I'm sure you all have some semi-decent ideas, too," Nebraska says, almost sincerely. "Let's hear them."

Manic Pixies always err on the side of positivity, and we cling to it even in our darkest hour. You can't keep a good Manic Pixie down. Now that we've had a moment to recover from Bridget's latest news, we're abuzz with suggestions on how we can win over the Council.

"We could build a hot air balloon and sprinkle glitter confetti all over Town Hall!" Mandy throws her hands up in a pantomime of said activity.

"We could teach the Stock Squirrels to tap dance and lead them in a Pixie parade!" Chloe breaks into a hyper version of her signature moves.

"Or we could decorate cymbals with murals depicting classic scenes from books that Manic Pixies have worked on!" Sky belts out in her best soprano.

Nebraska whistles to get our attention. "I admire everyone's enthusiasm. It reminds me how privileged we are to be part of the best Trope ever. And it gives me the most brilliant idea!" I certainly did not underestimate Nebraska's capacity to believe she has the *best* solution for everything.

Zelda fans the flames of Nebraska's vanity. "Do tell!"

"I propose a Manic Pixie *Pixie-Off*." With the level of mania shining in her baby blues, Nebraska is clearly the one to beat. "Our defense to the Council will be to go on a major charm offensive—to stage a friendly competition to showcase the utter originality of our creative talents. We will convince the Council that without us, the world of fiction would be a dull, dreary place, and they will rue the day they ever considered retiring us."

"Let's hear it for the Pixie-Off!" George cheers and follows up with a back handspring. If Nebraska can fire up George, then I have hope we can do the same for the Council.

"Hear, hear!" I chime in, and the others follow suit.

Angela promises to assist in any way she can. "I can start by doing some research into retirement trials—find out if any Trope has ever actually successfully changed the Council's mind and what strategies they used."

Angela truly is turning into our most enthusiastic ally. I'm not sure if New Age Therapists are programmed to be *this* supportive, but I appreciate it.

"Well, off you all go to brainstorm," Nebraska says, effectively kicking us out of her house. She blows us air kisses. "See you tomorrow."

Angela heads off to Shakespeare Marlowe Memorial Library, and the rest of us convene at Ooh La Latte Café for an emergency meeting. I order an entire pecan pie from the harried barista. Zelda orders the tea of the day, Positivi-tea. We could probably all use a dose of it.

At our table, George stabs her gooey slice like she wants to murder it. "Look, I'm thrilled we convinced Nebraska to include us, but I have to say, I think there's a high chance she'll end up screwing us over."

It's true that Nebraska's ego doesn't make her the ideal team player. But given George's shaky history with our Legacy

Pixie, it's possible she's overly suspicious. "She'd have nothing to gain from undermining us," I point out. "We're just trying to help save the Trope."

"That's what I mean, though," says George. "Nebraska doesn't care about saving the Trope. She only cares about herself. And as Legacy, she'll probably angle for special treatment, so she doesn't end up like the rest of us."

"Then we need to perform well in front of the Council," I insist. "We need to show them that we're all just as special as Nebraska. We can't let her show us up."

Mandy gasps. "Or *we* could sabotage *her.*"

George's eyes light up. "Oooh! How?"

The suggestions come fast and furious, which goes to show how much Nebraska has pissed these girls off:

"Shoot her with a super-soaker full of green food coloring!"

"Put ladybugs in all her pockets!"

"Set loose a carton of albino mice!"

Unfortunately, all of these ideas are far too whimsical to actually be effective, and I say so.

"Riley is right." George slumps into her seat. "We need to think outside the MPDG box. We need to make Nebraska look *boring.* Compared to the rest of us, at least."

It seems like an impossible feat. I've got nothing.

"None of us are experts in boring." Sky taps her ever-present headphones. "Can we find a consultant somewhere?"

"How about Clark?" Chloe jokes.

Mandy sticks her tongue out at Chloe. "You're hilarious."

I can't help but snicker. "They do say every joke begins with a kernel of truth. Maybe Clark *could* help us."

"You guys! Clark is not that bad."

Chloe groans. "Don't tell me you're back together again."

Mandy's sheepish expression gives her away.

"Oh, Mandy," goes the collective sigh.

Mandy serves herself the last slice of pie and takes a huge bite. She doesn't speak until she swallows. "Fine. I'll ask him for advice. But you all know that means I can't break up with him while he's helping us."

"Are you going to break up with him as part of our victory celebration?" Chloe asks.

Mandy sets down her plate and goes still. As much as she's been trying to be a good sport about our ribbing of Clark, it appears to have finally gotten to her. My protective instincts kick in.

"How about we concentrate on the Pixie-Off," I suggest. "We only have five days to prepare after all."

"Here's to saving our Trope!" Sky raises her forkful of pie.

"And to sticking it to Nebraska!" George squeals with such manic enthusiasm that even Mandy has to join in our laughter.

And the countdown begins.

CHAPTER 35

Zelda and I linger after the others skip out of the café. She's on her third Postivi-tea, but based on her gloomy expression, it doesn't seem to be helping. "I don't think we're taking this seriously enough," she complains to me. "These may be our last five days in TropeTown."

Her words put a serious dent in my manic energy. If we can't convince the Council we're worth keeping around, these may be the last five days I have with Zelda. I reject this possibility with all my being. "The Pixie-Off will work. It has to."

"But what if it doesn't? I would love to believe there is a future for us . . ." And the way she says "us" makes me think she means her and me "us," and my heart soars despite all the heaviness holding it down. "But realistically, planting may be our only option."

"It's not so dire yet that we have to do something that drastic," I insist. If she plants, there will definitely be no *us*.

She stirs her tea, clanking the spoon against the sides of the mug. "My current novel is not the worst novel in the world. I like Chet . . ."

"But you wouldn't be happy."

"Maybe I could learn to be? He's a good guy—he's complex, you know? An athlete *and* a scholar. He has all these big ideas for his life."

Maybe I could have big ideas for my life, too, if I thought I had any sort of control over it. TropeTown decides what work I do, whom I'm not allowed to date, and now whether I get to continue existing in the present tense.

She sighs. "Speaking of Chet—"

Suddenly my Author summons lights up. "Sorry—hold that thought, okay?" I can't help being a little relieved I don't have to hear anything else about Chet.

"See you later," she says as I fade out.

Once I recover from my jump and look up from my pitcher of water, I notice Ava's red-rimmed and puffy eyes. She's either been crying or she has serious seasonal allergies.

"What's wrong?" I pull her into a hug. She snuggles into my chest, and I'm surprised by how right it feels to hold her like this and comfort her. Even after Zelda basically hinted my hopes may not be in vain. What is wrong with me? My brain knows that love triangles are the worst, but try telling my body that.

"Rafferty and I had a fight."

"In the novel?" I rub circles on her lower back.

"There, too, but that's just manufactured drama. Off-Page."

How they live after the book is finished probably has a lot to do with how detailed the Author was with the setting. Marsden's house is so far no more than the barest outline of a sketch. Would I even have a roof over my head if I had to plant here?

"You two hang out a lot?" My voice sounds shrill, a clear indication I must like Ava more than I've admitted to myself.

Still in my arms, she leans back and peers up at me, her eyebrow arching at the exact angle Zelda's does. "We don't have a whole town, like you do. Just a bunkhouse during the work-in-progress phase. But Rafferty actually doesn't socialize much. He mostly plays video games. Blasting away at imaginary enemies all night long."

"That's annoying."

"Which is why I asked him to keep it down, and he blew up at me." She sighs. "Most days he's fine, really, but he can be so volatile if he doesn't get his way."

"That sounds manipulative and abusive."

Ava shakes her head. "Oh no, I didn't mean to give you the wrong impression. He doesn't hit me or anything like that. And sometimes he can be really sweet."

I don't like this situation one bit, but I feel powerless to do anything about it. It's not like I can pull her out of her own novel and take her back to TropeTown. If I planted here to escape the threat of retirement, I could take care of her—but would she even want that?

"Well, you deserve better," I say, finally. Because she does. "You deserve someone who respects you at all times, not just when it's convenient."

"Someone like you?" she asks so softly, I get a lump in my throat.

I pull her closer to my chest and kiss the top of her head. "I'm not really known for being the kind of guy who sticks around. There are better guys out there, I assure you."

"I don't know any of them." She sniffles, and I'm afraid I made her cry again. I'm supposed to be cheering her up. But I can't tell her she'll meet other guys, because it's up to her Author to create or hire them. There are other guy characters in her novel, but I'm not sure how much personality they have. Rafferty has a few buddies with names and lines, but I don't know anything about them and couldn't recommend them based on the company they keep.

As I contemplate what I can possibly say to her, the green light blinks on. We're suddenly joined by Rafferty and a crowd of extras and swept onto the soundstage. It's a complicated and chaotic scene involving Marsden organizing the school's marching band to play a current popular upbeat love song to Ava while she's running around the track with her gym class.

I start off by running down the bleachers while simultaneously singing into a microphone. Rafferty, who is sitting in the front row, trips me as I come past, but I do a flip in the air and land triumphantly on my feet. Everyone cheers, except for Rafferty, obviously.

Ava runs up to me, and I spin her around to the music while the rest of her gym class acts as back-up dancers. It's exhilarating to have this victory. Ava's eyes never leave mine, and her entire face is lit up in incandescent joy. I'm suddenly struck by the thought that if I planted here, I could relive this moment over and over. Could such happiness ever get old?

The entire production is cut short by the Errant Gym Teacher finally returning to class and blowing his whistle. In the aftermath, the teacher condemns both Ava and Rafferty to detention, which ruins Ava's plans to hang out with Marsden. While Ava is disappointed, Rafferty rubs his hands together in eager anticipation of getting Ava alone.

"Tough luck, chap." Rafferty bumps my shoulder as he leads Ava to the sidelines. The soundstage is reset for their detention scene, and Ava blows me a kiss behind Rafferty's back.

As she's pulled away from me, the achy spot in my heart grows a little bigger.

Lingering at the craft services table, I allow myself to imagine what it might be like to live full-time in Ava's novel. The way things are going between us, it seems like Ava would choose me Off-Page even if her Author is #TeamRafferty. But no matter how deeply Ava and I might end up loving each other, Rafferty will always lurk in the background. Every time a Reader follows Ava's story, I would have to see Ava kissing Rafferty On-Page. I'm not even the jealous kind, but I defy anyone to say that doesn't suck.

Not to mention I'd be cut off from Zelda and all my Manic Pixie friends. They might plant in equally sub-par scenarios—or else they'd be retired.

There has to be another way.

CHAPTER 36

The next morning, we attend un-therapy at Nebraska's, and we spend so much time working on our plans for the Pixie-Off, I never get a chance to look for Finn's letter. And yet it doesn't feel like we're making much progress. Nebraska keeps telling us whatever we do has to be spontaneous or it will seem too stiff. Which seems to add credibility to our fears that she's actually coming up with her own plan to save only herself—leaving us to flounder and fall prey to the Council's wrath.

Angela does have one helpful suggestion: that we rally the rest of TropeTown's Manic Pixies to attend the hearing, even though they can't all be part of the Pixie-Off. Having them there for moral support and to demonstrate the diversity of our Trope might win us some points with the Council.

It's going to take the better part of the four days we have left to track down all 150 of our fellow Pixies, and the prospect doesn't raise our spirits—especially since, at the moment, it seems like we might be inviting them to their own funeral. As we morosely shuffle out of TropeTown Heights, Mandy claps her hands together to get our attention. "So Clark said he's willing to help us find a way to make Nebraska seem boring . . ."

We cheer.

"... provided we allow him to give us all a tour of the glass factory."

We jeer.

"Boring!" Chloe whines.

"Yes!" George shimmies in her hot pants. "Which makes him the perfect man for the job!"

"So when are we going?" Sky asks.

Mandy throws up her hands in the air, as if we've won a grand prize. "Right now!"

On the way to the glass factory, Zelda and I trail the other girls by a decent enough distance for the illusion of privacy. She bumps up against my shoulder and casually touches my arm to point out signs along the road that she finds funny. We wrap ourselves in a cocoon of conspiratorial coziness, and I can't get enough of it.

While the other girls spread their zany cheer among random pedestrians, Zelda sticks close to me. "Riley," she whispers, "I was wondering ... will you come to work with me later? I need your help."

"You mean, jump into your Novel with you? Is that even possible?"

She nods solemnly. I don't shake her down for logistical details. There's no rule against this as far as I know, but then again, I've never heard of anyone trying it, either.

Still, if Zelda needs my help, I'm going to be there for her. "Of course."

She lets out a sigh of relief. "I'm lucky to have someone like you." Her words are so reminiscent of Ava's that I do a double take. I close my eyes for split second and I see Ava, and the lump in my throat returns as well. My chest swirls with guilt and confusion and nervousness. I don't want to feel these negative emotions. I want them to go away. I push them down and pull on a smile. I grab Zelda's hand and rush up with her to the rest of group, letting their stream of mindless chatter and laughter cure me.

When we enter the Industrial District, our convivial rowdiness garners disapproving stares from workers in orange hard hats. Mandy and Sky try to look dignified for about five seconds before they throw up their hands and start skipping.

From the outside, the factory looks more like a gothic cathedral than an industrial building. The massive structure features three semicircular arches in the front and is topped by two towers with slit windows.

Clark greets us at the wrought-iron door and ushers us inside to a vestibule area lined by wooden benches. He puts his arm around Mandy. "Welcome to the tour, ladies. And Riley."

"Not so fast," George says. "Before we begin, we want to hear your strategy for solving our problem."

Mandy shrugs out of his embrace. "Yes, Clark. What have you prepared for us on the topic of being boring?"

"Other than taking us on this pathetic tour," Chloe chimes in under her breath.

Clark tugs at the sleeve of his thick, plaid work shirt. "Well, I know how you all appreciate whimsy, so I will reveal my plan at the end of the tour, kind of like how a leprechaun gives you a pot of treasure when you follow his rainbow."

Clark has more insight into the Manic Pixie psyche than I would have given him credit for. I slow clap my appreciation, and the girls join me in my applause, even Chloe (grudgingly).

"Thank you," Clark says. "Now let's begin."

Past the vestibule, the space opens up into high vaulted ceilings crisscrossed by exposed beams and pipes. Clark tells us that the pane work is done in an adjacent building in the back, which is off limits. No complaints from us.

We gather around an active glassblowing session. A man in coveralls stands on a two-foot-high platform with a long tube, while another man sits below him tending a furnace that's enclosed in a thin, black cylinder about the thickness of one of Clark's legs. Coveralls rotates the tube and pulls molten glass out with it, which he carries over to a steel table to shape.

Clark describes the process in all its minutiae, throwing around terms like *marver* and *jacks* and *punty*. And by the end, Coveralls has created an elegant clear vase.

"Any questions?" Clark asks us.

"Where's our treasure?" Chloe asks. If her eyes were any more glazed over, they could be served at a doughnut shop.

"Tour isn't over!" He grins, and I wonder if all we're getting at the end of this rainbow is a pot full of fool's gold.

We move on to the storage racks, rows of steel shelves that hold thousands upon thousands of glass pieces in every color. At one end of the racks, a heavy yellow ladder leads up to a balcony.

"Ooh, can we climb up there?" Chloe brushes back her bangs. It's the first smidgen of interest she's shown since we got here, but Clark seems hesitant to allow it.

"I need to ask the supervisor on duty. Be right back."

While we wait, Sky and George decide to stage a mini-musical under the balcony. Using the ladder as a support, they fling themselves to and fro while making up silly lyrics that they sing in operatic style. Chloe and Mandy join in the dance action while Zelda and I stomp out a drumbeat from the sidelines.

As Chloe, George, and Mandy all swing around the ladder

at the same time, we hear a loud crack, and the ladder separates itself from the balcony and falls toward the first storage rack. All the girls and I back away to a safe distance, which is why none of us gets hurt when the ladder smashes into the shelf. This sets up a chain reaction that topples over the storage racks like dominos.

To our credit, we all hang our heads and cringe, pressing our hands over our ears. Still, the sound of crashing glass will likely follow me to my grave.

I clap Mandy on the shoulder. "Well, maybe Clark will break up with you now."

Clark rushes over to us. His lower lip wobbles in disbelief.

I brace myself for screaming, but he doesn't say a word, which is somehow worse. He's never going to share his plan with us now. Not that I'd blame him.

"We didn't mean to do it." Mandy puts out her palms in supplication. "The ladder must have been loose."

He hugs her and inspects her for cuts. "I'm just happy you're okay. You're not hurt, are you?"

"No. I'm fine."

"We can't stay here. C'mon." He grabs Mandy's hand, and she takes mine, and I hold Zelda's. The other girls latch on until we are a human chain picking a path through forests of glass.

When we reach the safety of the vestibule, we sit on a wooden bench, and Clark paces back and forth in front of us. "My boss will not be happy about this. He'll never let me give tours again! Especially not to your kind."

"We accept this punishment," Chloe says, slightly too eagerly. I have to bite my lip to keep from snickering.

"Tell us your plan, honey," Mandy says in a silky tone, "and we'll be out of here lickety-split."

He sighs and stops pacing. "Fine. So Mandy says that Nebraska thinks very highly of herself . . ."

"A truer statement was never uttered," Sky says. "Nebraska is so self-important that she cuts to the front of every line."

Zelda chimes in. "Nebraska is so stuck-up that when she walks into parties, she makes the host announce her entrance."

"Oooh!" I say. "I have one. Nebraska is so vain, she probably thinks this conversation is about her."

Chloe harrumphs. "Nebraska is so vain, she thinks *every* conversation is about her."

Mandy puts up her hand. "All true, but let's let Clark speak, you guys."

"So I was thinking . . ." Clark rubs his chin with his index finger. "Bragging is boring, right?"

George whoops. "So boring!"

Clark accepts her validation with a curt nod. "All you have to do is convince her to talk about herself. A lot."

CHAPTER 37

After marveling at the simple genius of Clark's plan, we hightail it out of the Industrial District before they can kick us out. Our friends get ready to fan out on a mission to invite TropeTown's other Manic Pixies to attend the Council meeting. Zelda and I make excuses for why we can't join them.

"I have to wash my hair," I claim.

"I . . . Uh . . . I have to wash my neighbor's hair," Zelda says. "She's a Sympathetic Elderly Shut-in . . ."

Mandy gives us a knowing look. "We'll fill you in on our progress tomorrow. If we make any."

Once the others are out of sight, Zelda fiddles with her band. "Are you ready to go with me now?"

"Do you mind telling me what this is all about first?"

"I heard a rumor about Reader World. And I want to ask Chet about it."

"Why can't you ask him at work?"

"Because this conversation needs to happen Off-Page, and he won't agree to do it because he doesn't take me seriously." Zelda scoots closer to me and puts her hand on my knee. "If I take you with me, he'll finally understand I mean business."

I don't have to remind her that while bringing a guest into

a Novel isn't against the rules, going Off-Page *is*. Merely suggesting it landed her in therapy. Actually doing it could merit termination. Our Trope is already in trouble. We don't need to give the Council another reason to retire us all. "Zelda, that's a huge risk. Are you sure following up on this rumor is worth it?"

Zelda's expression hardens. "Finn thought so."

"Wait—what does Finn have to do with this?"

"He's the source of the rumor."

And just like that, I'm back in again.

"So what *is* the rumor?" Apparently Finn confided something to her that he didn't to me.

She glances around the room nervously, as if she thinks someone may be watching. "Not here. Off-Page."

"Fine." I try to hide my annoyance. It's not Zelda's fault Finn kept so many secrets from his supposed best friend.

She threads her fingers through mine and pulls a lever on the side of her band. The Author summons light pulses. And we're off.

We land and immediately rehydrate. Fortunately, the backstage area is the standard format, familiar to me down to the placement of the craft services table and its assortment of pies.

A guy dressed in full-on football gear approaches. "Zelda?"

"Hi, Chet," Zelda says brightly.

He whips out a clipboard. "You're not on the schedule today."

Chet doesn't look at all like I pictured him. He doesn't have horns or a pointy tail, just a quizzical expression and brown hair. He carries a helmet. I remember Zelda explaining that she admired him because he wasn't some dumb jock. That he had aspirations.

"I came to see you." Zelda throws her arms around him and buries her head in his chest. He lets his free hand tangle her hair, and oh geez, does it hurt to see them like this, even though I know it's her job, and she's also buttering him up to get a favor. Maybe she'd hate to see the way I act with Ava, too.

"Who is this guy?" Chet asks. "He's not on the schedule either."

Zelda lets go of Chet and moves back to my side. "He wouldn't be. He's not a character in this novel. He's my friend from TropeTown. Riley."

The word 'friend' wounds me further.

Chet looks torn. I recognize the anguish of simultaneously yearning to protect someone you love and yet give them what they want. "Zelda, no. We talked about this. We can't."

Zelda takes his helmet from him. "Just give us a few minutes. Please. And I'll never bring it up again."

He shakes his head, and I brace myself for his refusal. Instead he relents and turns to lead us through the door marked "Private." The one that has never opened for me until now.

CHAPTER 38

I wish I could tell you what we talked about Off-Page. The rumor, if true, changes everything we thought we knew about the choices we have. It shakes the very foundations of TropeTown.

I can't tell you though. Not yet, at least. You're reading this, so that means anyone could be.

I can tell you that the rumor is so fantastical, I can't imagine it being true. And it's so fantastic, I hope with all my being that it is.

It's worth noting that Chet doesn't believe it. And by the end of our conversation, Zelda seems equally skeptical. But I want to believe.

I'm beginning to suspect having this knowledge is what put Finn on the Termination Train.

And it means I'm even more desperate to get my hands on his letter to Nebraska.

CHAPTER 39

When I walk out of my apartment the next morning, fretting because we only have three days to prepare our defense, Zelda stands near the tree looking up at Sprite.

"I came to pick you up, and Sprite zipped by me."

"She's showing off. Because she likes you so much."

I show off, too—and for the same reason—by climbing to retrieve Sprite.

Once I deliver Sprite safely back to Crazy Cat Lady Cathy, Zelda and I head off to TropeTown Heights for our un-therapy.

"So," I say. "That rumor. Do you think . . ."

"Shhhh," Zelda warns sharply. And her expression says the rest.

We continue the rest of the way in silence, Zelda kicking at a stone. I want to assure her everything will be fine, but I don't want to be liar, so I keep my mouth shut.

The guard lets us in without incident. He checks our names off the list and waves us through.

We round the corner of Nebraska's house and climb the steps to the veranda, side by side. We must see Bridget at the same time, because Zelda stumbles and catches herself on my arm so she doesn't trip. She digs her fingernails in, and I know she's as terrified as I am, though she's trying not to show it.

Bridget stares at us with an accusatory expression. "Your stragglers have finally arrived, Angela. And now I can state my business."

Holy crap. She knows.

Angela smiles through chattering teeth. "Okay, Bridget. Why don't you have some pie! I baked it myself. Boysenberry."

"No, thank you," Bridget says.

"Don't mind if I do!" Nebraska gets up to serve herself a piece of pie, and Bridget waits patiently for her to finish.

Meanwhile, Zelda and I sit down. George whispers something to Mandy, and Mandy nods, folding her hands in her lap and looking resigned to her fate. The other girls probably think Bridget's visit has to do with our accident at the glass factory, and not with Zelda's and my rule breaking.

Maybe it's neither.

Maybe it's both.

But Bridget has already threatened our very existence in TropeTown. How much worse can it get?

Bridget clears her throat. "As you all know, our community functions because we follow the rules. And when someone doesn't follow the rules, it puts our peace in jeopardy. We can't condone this type of behavior."

My whole body blares an alert. My muscles tense and I can't get enough air in my lungs. Why did we have to go Off-Page? Now they will terminate us immediately, and we'll never know the truth. Zelda's nails find the tender skin of my arm again.

Bridget pulls a plastic evidence bag out of the pocket of her suit jacket. A charred black mess rests inside the bag.

"Our forensics team determined the fire in the Healing Center started with this item. Does anyone recognize it?"

As Bridget waves the bag in our faces, my rapid breathing slows down a notch. Bridget didn't come for Zelda and me.

But George gasps. "That's my friendship bracelet."

Angela clamps her hand over her mouth so hard, we can hear the smack.

Bridget stalks over to George's chair. "So, Georgina . . . you confess?"

"No . . . I . . . lost it," George stammers.

Bridget clicks her tongue. "Witnesses have come forward with statements placing you outside the Healing Center very early on the morning of the fire."

George whips around to face Nebraska. "Nebraska and I met up for a chat. Go on, tell them!"

Nebraska's eyes widen in innocence. "Why would I meet you somewhere voluntarily? *Everyone* knows we avoid each other at all costs."

When she puts it that way, George's story does seem unlikely.

"We used to be friends," George fires back. "Before I told you I was being considered for a promotion. And now you've set me up. All because you couldn't stand someone else sharing your Legacy limelight."

This, however, seems incredibly likely.

Sky shakes her head like she's been betrayed. "Why did you never tell me about this, George?"

George opens her mouth to speak, but Angela interrupts. "Stop this right now," she commands, her voice trembling slightly. "Your Trope is in enough trouble, without you bringing unsubstantiated accusations against your *sole* Legacy member."

The sparkle fades from George's eyes, which tells me she catches Angela's warning as well as I do. If George takes down Nebraska with her, she leaves us without a Legacy member to speak for us. The Council won't listen to the rest of us on our own, and we won't get a chance to prove ourselves.

"I'm so sorry," she says finally, hanging her head.

Bridget takes this as a confession. "Come with me."

"But where are you taking her?" Sky demands.

"To the Villain Zone."

CHAPTER 40

The Villain Zone, like the Termination Train, is shrouded in mystery and rumors. None of us have ever been there, of course. It's off-limits to non-Villainous Tropes, with the exception of Council Members and Legacies.

Speaking of Legacies, ours seems to be taking George's arrest in stride. She is sipping at her sweet tea with a sparkle in her eye. The rest of us, not so much.

Angela dismisses us early due to the circumstances and heads out alone into the trees behind Nebraska's property. We're all so upset that we leave without even tasting the boysenberry pie.

It's only once we've reached the border of Nebraska's property and escaped the heavy film of her gloating that I remember my plan to retrieve Finn's letter. That'll have to wait until our next un-therapy session.

Mandy invites us to vent at her apartment.

"Poor George!" Sky flings herself down on Mandy's aubergine velvet sofa. "Nebraska is the worst!"

"Yeah, but unfortunately we need her," Mandy says, stating the obvious. She and Chloe join Sky on the sofa, and Zelda and I take the armchairs opposite. If George were here, one of us would have to sit on the floor. It's a painful realization that we might never get to hang out with her again.

"I don't understand why George never told any of us about this Legacy thing," Sky says. "And yet she told Nebraska, of all people."

Chloe fiddles with the hem of her bright neon green frock. "She probably freaked out and had a lapse in judgment. You know how she gets under pressure."

Yeah, the same as all of us Manic Pixies get when stressed out—hyper and irrational. We could all use a major dose of Angela telling us to chill.

"George probably told Nebraska in the hopes of getting some advice," Zelda adds, "but then Nebraska hated the idea of George living next door to her and having all the same privileges."

"How can we help her?" Mandy asks miserably. She applies a fresh coat of red lipstick, as if that might cheer her up. "She basically sacrificed herself for the good of the Trope. We can't let her waste away in the VZ."

"But it's not as if we can break her out of jail," I say. "The only people we know who could even get us into the VZ are Bridget and Nebraska." Neither seems likely to volunteer for such a mission. I suppose I could try to ingratiate myself with Sal the collie, but asking such a self-centered character for a favor doesn't seem like a promising option either.

Sky raises her hand. "Maybe we can't help George right now, but we can make sure we do our best at the Pixie-Off."

"Agreed," says Zelda. "If we prove our Trope deserves to live on, maybe the Council will be willing to revisit George's case. But if we can't convince the Council to spare us, we'll all be retired, including George."

Sky nods. "George gave us this chance to make our case to the Council, and it's what she would want us to do."

"Well, she'd also want us to upstage Nebraska," Chloe says. "Where are we on Clark's suggestion to ensure Nebraska brags about herself? Any ideas?"

Sky jumps up and windmills like she's Pete Townshend on guitar. Her headphones bounce against her neck. "I got it! I can collaborate with Nebraska on a song proclaiming her greatness."

Mandy brightens slightly. "That's a good idea, but you don't think Nebraska will be suspicious if you're suddenly helping her? She's not stupid."

"That's why I need to have a falling out with all of you," Sky says. "And then I'll become Nebraska's biggest fan."

CHAPTER 41

We pinkie swear on Sky's plan, which will go into effect at our next un-therapy session. Outside Mandy's house, everyone heads off in separate directions except Zelda and me. I quickly try to gauge whether she wants my company. She's not cozying up to me, but she hasn't been shutting me out either, so it's hard to tell.

I offer her my arm, and she smiles and takes it. I start to feel more confident, and I decide we could both use a distraction from all the crud weighing us down.

"Maybe now's a good time to catch me up on comics," I suggest. "We could go hang out in the mall, and you can help me decide if I want to commit to the Jazz-Hands Spider-Mouse universe or the Razzle-Dazzle Spider-Mouse universe. I'll have you know I'm partial to the Razzle-Dazzle."

She stiffens and unhooks herself from me. "Really, Riley? Our friend has just been wrongly accused and carted off to jail, and our whole Trope is in danger of retirement, and all you care about is pandering to me so that maybe I'll make out with you?"

I mean, she's not wrong about the making-out part, but I'm rather offended that she'd accuse me of being so callous. "Hey, I'm just as worried as you are! I've spent the last few days thinking about how to help our Trope survive. And I went with you to investigate that rumor—"

"Riley!" she says sharply, before dropping her voice to a whisper. "Never mind the rumor. It's merely wishful thinking—talking to Chet confirmed that for me. There's no point in dwelling on it when we have real problems."

"Well, there's nothing more we can do about our real problems right now either. So what's wrong with giving ourselves a breather?"

"Ugh! Men! You can only handle so much emotional strain before you run for cover." Her eyes flash with righteous fury. "And here I deluded myself into thinking you were special."

Hold up. She thinks I'm special? Holy freaking hallelujah! But did I just blow it?

"Soooo you'd go on a date with me?" I blurt, because I'm an idiot and don't know when to keep my mouth shut. And also, I really want to know.

She glances at me shyly and her cheeks erupt pink. She opens and closes her mouth. She's flustered, and Zelda has never once been rendered speechless in my presence. It's not who she is. She crosses and uncrosses her arms over her chest and looks down. "We can't."

Which isn't the same as an "I don't want to," so I forge ahead. "Why not?"

"Riley," she says, her voice hitching, "*why* are you asking me out?" Her gaze rises tentatively to meet mine.

I wait a minute to answer, because I'm terrified to tell her the truth. But if I never risk anything, I can never reap the rewards either. "Because I think I may be in love with you."

She smiles wistfully and shakes her head. "You're not in love with me."

I'm about to insist that I am, but something stops me. I have to admit I don't really know what love is. I've been programmed to pursue the romantic trappings of it, but I suppose I haven't spent much time considering what I would want or need from an actual relationship.

"If anything," Zelda goes on, "you're in love with the concept of me. You don't even know me. Because the real me—heck, even I don't know who that is."

I suddenly notice she's not wearing one of her pins today—almost like she's given up on her search for identity. "But does anyone really have all that figured out? I bet not even Developeds do. Or even Readers."

She takes off her glasses and slips them in her pocket. Without them, she looks younger and more delicate. "I don't actually need these. I have perfect vision. I wear them because they make me feel fierce."

"You *are* fierce," I confirm.

"I am. But I'm also a coward. I'm generous, but I'm also selfish. I'm smart, but I can't tell the difference between left and right."

I lift my left hand. "Quick, which hand am I holding up?"

She grabs it. "This one."

My breath catches in my throat. "Cheater," I whisper.

"See?" She takes a step closer. "I have lots of undesirable qualities. Do you still want to ask me out?"

"I do."

We stare at each other, and it's so intense I think I might faint.

She crosses her eyes. "Even now?"

"Now, especially."

Her eyes crinkle at the edges, and she looks like she's

trying very hard to suppress a grin. "I'm thinking I could kiss you right now . . ."

Oh my god. It's happening.

I lean in eagerly, but she coughs, and I freeze mid-swoop.

". . . but I also think now would be the wrong time. I mean, 95 percent of my brain is occupied by the thought that we might not exist as of next week . . . and honestly, Riley, you deserve more than 5 percent of my attention."

I step back to give her space. I want to kiss her, but I also want her to be more than 5 percent into it.

"I'm confident we are going to rock the Council with our Pixie-Off," I say, exaggerating slightly. "So I can wait."

She hugs me and giggles into my shoulder. "I admire your restraint."

"Why thank you." I curtsey with her still clinging to me, so it's somewhat awkward. "I've won several awards for it. Did you notice them gleaming on my shelf?"

"I think I was too busy sneaking glances at you," she says, and my heart shoots off fireworks.

I can be patient. I can be patient. I can be patient.

But I have to untangle myself from her to do it. So I do. And I think of the least sexy thing I can say right now.

"Look, I'm going to make it my mission to free George, okay?"

"No," she says and puts her glasses back on.

"No?"

She reinitiates contact by lacing her fingers through mine. "Let's make it *our* mission to free George."

CHAPTER 42

Before Zelda and I can plot a course that will take us to the VZ to save George, I get an Author summons.

I point at my band apologetically, and Zelda leans over and gives me a kiss on the cheek, so obviously I am never washing my cheek again. "See you later," she says. "I'll be at the pool hall if you want to meet up."

I hate leaving her, but I have to. I take a deep breath and press my summons button.

Backstage is dark when I land, and I can barely find my way around. All there is to drink is a pitcher of metallic-tasting water, but I guzzle it down anyway.

What the heck is going on? Why did I get a summons if the Author isn't writing today?

Finally, the door marked "Private" squeaks open, and Ava comes in holding a flashlight and a pie. She bounds over to me and sits down, handing me the pie with a flourish.

"I baked this just for you," she declares, smiling like a goof. "Rhubarb."

"What's the occasion?" I wipe a bit of flour from her nose.

"I missed you," she explains, like it's the most obvious fact in the world. "And I know you love pie."

I take a bite. It's perfect and I tell her so.

"Thank you," she says. "I burned the first couple I attempted, but if at first you don't succeed . . ."

"Never give up."

"We need to tell that to the Author." Ava clicks the flashlight on and off, pointing it at the closed soundstage. "She hasn't written a word since you were last here. She thinks the novel is a mess and that she's a huge failure."

"So the Author didn't call me to work today?"

"No, I called you. And not only because I missed you. Because I think you can help."

"Help? How?" I'm honestly at a loss.

"You're a Manic Pixie." Ava shines the flashlight at my face but is careful to avoid blinding my eyes. "It's your job to light up people's lives, right? Maybe you can convince the Author she's on the right track. Give her faith in herself again."

I can't suppress an ironic laugh. Me? The boy on probation for not trusting my Authors is supposed to help an Author regain her inner trust?

"What's wrong?" Ava asks.

"I wish the TropeTown council believed in Manic Pixies as much as you do." I place the pie under my chair. I take the flashlight from her and point it at the ground. "Our Trope is currently in danger of being retired."

"But why?" She clutches my arm like I might immediately disappear. "Don't they get how much the world needs you?"

"We have one last chance to try to make them understand." I tell her about the fire and George being hauled away as well as about the Council meeting and our plans for the Pixie-Off. While I talk, she rubs circles into my wrist.

"I'd stand up in front of the council and defend you if I

could," Ava declares. We both know she can't actually do this. If she ventured into TropeTown even for a quick visit, her novel would collapse without her.

"Thanks. That means a lot."

"Have you thought about planting here?" she asks tentatively. Her fingers tense as she waits for my answer.

"It's an option." I'm careful to keep my tone neutral. The truth is it might turn out to be the lesser evil, but that still doesn't make it a great choice for me personally. "I really like spending time with you."

"And isn't the Author doing a fantastic job of world-building and crafting scenes?" she prompts me with a wink.

"If she could create someone as wonderful as you, Ava," I say truthfully, "she has to have massive talent."

The lights blaze back on just in time for me to catch Ava blushing. She immediately looks away from me, up at the bright fluorescents. "You did it!" she squeals. "You're awesome, Riley! And you should never, ever be retired." She jumps onto my lap and kisses me all over my face in gratitude. I feel an unfamiliar pride in making a real impact and being appreciated for it.

With our Author back in business, we get called in to work on a scene where Ava presses Marsden to define their relationship. It's after midnight, and Marsden has climbed the trellis and wriggled himself through Ava's bedroom window. They both wear pajamas, and Marsden has a serious case of bedhead. They sit on top of her frilly pink bedspread, an oddly sentimental decorating choice for the usually no-nonsense Ava.

MARSDEN: Hey, I thought maybe we could ride our bikes to the grocery store and buy some cinnamon Pop-Tarts.

AVA: In our pajamas?

MARSDEN: Obvs. It's more fun that way.

AVA: Can't. When they induced vomiting at the vet, Bruiser totally ruined my sneakers.

MARSDEN: You must have more shoes!

AVA: Well, yeah, but not any others with sufficient grip to safely scale the trellis.

MARSDEN: Barefoot?

AVA: It's too early in our relationship to show you my feet.

MARSDEN: Oh? When does the big foot reveal usually come, in your experience?

AVA: After you actually define the relationship.

MARSDEN: So you mean, if I say 'Hey, Ava—is it cool if I call you my girlfriend?' you respond by flashing me your pedicure?

AVA: Something like that, yeah.

MARSDEN: Hmmm . . . good to know.

AVA: So do you want to see my feet?

MARSDEN: I didn't have that particular interest until recently.

AVA (giggles): I'm pulling down a sock . . .

MARSDEN: Oh my! Exposed ankle!

AVA: Seriously though . . .

MARSDEN (gets down on his knees in front of Ava's bed):
Ava, I wish for you to accompany me on a barefoot quest in
search of sugary sustenance. Will you accept my proposal
and make me the giddiest man in all the land?

AVA: I accept.

The scene continues with Ava and Marsden carrying out
their plan and having sweet moments together, both literally
and figuratively. The drama comes when the store manager
won't let them shop without shoes, but then Marsden comes up
with the great plan of buying flip-flops from the front seasonal
display. Crisis averted!

After the scene finishes, Ava and I return to our seats to
gorge ourselves on her rhubarb pie.

"I had so much fun with you today," Ava says.

"Actually, you had so much fun with Marsden."

"You could be Marsden, you know," she says, pointedly
alluding to our earlier conversation about planting.

"It's just . . . I don't want to be Marsden." I put down my
fork. "I want to be Riley."

"What's the big difference?" she asks, and not all snarky,
but like she really doesn't get it. She's never had to pretend to
be someone else, so I guess I can't expect her to understand how
easily the lines between reality and fiction can blur if you stop

paying attention. How easily you can lose yourself.

I don't know how to answer her question, so I deflect with a question of my own. "Are you happy?"

She takes another bite of pie, but I can't. My stomach gurgles at the thought of it.

"Remember that Inspiring Teacher Trope who has done a few scenes with me? She told me happiness is knowing your purpose. And I do. My Author created me for the express purpose of living in this story. I wouldn't exist otherwise."

"And my purpose is to fulfil my Trope duties to the best of my ability," I sigh. "But that doesn't feel like enough."

"I'm no expert on Tropes, but maybe the whole idea is that you try on all these different roles until you find one that fits you best."

"But what if the role that fits me best is Riley?" I muse aloud.

I don't expect her to answer, but she does. "Then find a way to be Riley. No matter what it takes."

CHAPTER 43

Lying on my sofa, I ponder Ava's parting words. Find a way to be Riley. It seems impossible. I get up and sharpen a jumbo box of pencils, which I send soaring one by one to puncture the ceiling with their pointy ends until an entire forest of cedar and graphite claims the space above me.

Even though it's late, I head outside because I need to burn off my nervous energy. My feet take me to the Entertainment District, and I revel in the thought of Zelda suckering some poor saps into games of pool they have no chance of winning. But when I get to the Wild West Saloon, the Muscle-Bound Bouncer blocks me from entering.

"We're closed. Scram." His bulging biceps cross his pecs like mating whales. I step back, intimidated. In comparison, my biceps resemble much less majestic creatures, like puffins.

Laughter from inside pours out into the alley, so not all the clientele has been kicked out yet.

"Is Zelda still here?"

He rubs his chin. "Should I tell you? You can't be a Creepy Stalker Dude, because you'd be locked down in the Villain Zone."

The doors swing open and Zelda emerges, kicking up a

dust cloud of peanut shells. "Don't give him a hard time, Vic. He's with me."

And as if to really drive home her point, she slips her arm around my waist and leans into me.

My outsides play it cool, but my insides are shooting off wild sparks. Zelda claims me. Her hand on my hip feels like a promise of delicious days and nights to come.

Vic reacts with a skeptical sneer. "This guy? Really? I bet he can't even hold a cue properly."

Zelda ruffles her other hand through my hair. "Eh, but he sure is hot!"

"If you say so." Vic gives me the tiniest of nods, but I don't need his approval—especially not when Zelda writes me poster-sized checks of validation.

She salutes him, and we walk.

"Did you mean that?" I ask. "You think I'm hot?"

"Duh. All Manic Pixies are hot," she says, and I'm reminded of saying something similar to Ava not that long ago. Right now, Ava seems impossibly distant, like a faded photograph tucked away in an attic. Ava is destined to be a memory, while Zelda is someone I have the chance to make memories with.

"Oh, clever way to fish for a compliment!" I tease.

She laughs and strikes a model pose. "You caught me."

"You're so hot, Zelda."

"Duh," she says, but I can tell that she's pleased I said so.

Since it's so late, most of the carnival workers that lurk around these parts have packed up and gone home already. But the basketball hoop challenge is still open, promising to reward winners with useless, oversized monstrosities.

Who could resist?

I swipe my card to buy ten throws from the young man running the booth. He passes me the first ball with flinty precision.

Zelda hoots in support, slapping my back like a good teammate. "You got this, Riley."

I square my feet and concentrate on my follow-through. Scoring is all about honing the fine motor skills of your fingertips, and my fingertips are more than ready to prove themselves.

"All net!" I pump my fist in victory.

I sink the next eight as well. Which if I'm true to my average, means I'll probably miss the last one.

The carnival guy's tosses to me have become increasingly erratic, as if he has been slowly acclimatizing to the notion of parting ways with a big prize. And the last ball misses me entirely and hits Zelda in the thigh.

"Why don't you give your girl a chance," he proposes slyly.

Zelda's not one to pass up a challenge, and she boxes me out when I go for the wayward ball. "I got this," she says.

"I trust you." The words rush out of my mouth, but once they escape, I realize they're true.

"Maybe it's a mistake to put too much faith in me." She dribbles the ball once, like a pro.

When the whole game's at stake, you can't second-guess yourself or you lose your nerve. "I made my choice, and I'm sticking it with it."

She gives me an appraising look with narrowed eyes and holds it a moment too long.

The carnival guy sees his opportunity and begins to heckle her. "You're going to screw this up for him. Mark my words."

Zelda palms the ball. "If I wanted bogus prophecy, I'd have gone to the Fortune Teller."

I assume a superhero stance to form a protective screen for her. She loosens up by performing a plié followed by a pirouette. "Okay," she says. "Here goes nothing."

She puts the ball up with both hands, not the best tactic. It hits the inside of the rim and rolls in a spin.

I hold my breath. Will it go in?

Finally it slows and drops, right through the net, and I exhale in a congratulatory puff. "You did it!"

"Close call, though." Her cheeks pink up in bright dots.

The carnival guy groans and reluctantly retrieves a giant hippo, a smaller cousin, perhaps, to the one at Nebraska's place. "Here. Take it."

Zelda and I hug the hippo between us. We both know we're not going to carry it all the way home, but we savor our success for a satisfying sixty seconds.

She lets go first, and I transfer ownership back to the bewildered carnival guy. "No thank you. We don't need trophies to know we're awesome."

"And anyway," Zelda says, "we prefer to collect experiences."

As we leave, I feel more like myself than I have in long time. I may only be a Trope, but at least I can make my own choices and memories while I'm free to roam TropeTown.

I can't plant. I need to stay and defend my Trope. I need to fight for my right to be me—even if I'm still figuring out who that really is.

CHAPTER 44

We've barely made it ten steps when my summons band lights up again.

"Your Author must be experiencing an unexpected bout of productivity," Zelda remarks. She seems disappointed that I have to go, which I chalk up as my second major win of the evening.

"We're at the end, I think. I bet she just wants to get it done."

"I'm glad you came by." Zelda hugs me, and I want to sink into it forever.

But I reluctantly step out of her embrace and press the button on my band. "See you soon."

The summons turns out to be for an all-nighter. When Ava asks me how I'm doing, I mutter that I'm fine and leave it at that. For now.

Because we need all the concentration we can muster, as the scene we're working on is Ava's "dark night of the soul" moment. Just as she's feeling comfortable choosing Marsden over Rafferty, Marsden gives her some shocking news. We do variations of the scene over and over, until the Author feels like she gets it right.

MARSDEN: I want to join the military.

AVA: What? Why?

MARSDEN: It's a chance to get out there and experience the world.

AVA: You couldn't hack it in the military. You have no respect for authority. They'd hate you and try to break your spirit every day.

MARSDEN: You make an excellent point. Okay, no military.

AVA (snuggles up to him): Staying with me is definitely the better option. We can go to college together and have a cute house with a white picket fence . . .

MARSDEN: Ava . . . you know I adore you . . . but I can't settle down until I find my true self.

AVA: But what if you go chasing after your true self and never find him, because he was here all along, and all you're doing is running away from him?

MARSDEN: It's a chance I have to take. Don't you get it? If I don't keep moving, I'll slowly wither. All the brightness you love will dim.

AVA: I don't want to lose you.

MARSDEN: You'll never lose me. I'll always be a part of you.

That doesn't change if I join the circus or become a roadie for a rock band or teach salsa dancing on a cruise ship in the Indian Ocean.

(Ava cries cathartically for ten minutes while Marsden rubs her back.)

MARSDEN: You could come with me.

AVA (sniffles): You know I can't. I'm not like you. I'm not spontaneous or free-spirited. My life doesn't fit in a backpack like yours does.

MARSDEN: You can do whatever you choose. That's the beauty of free will.

AVA (takes a steadying breath): I get that. But my choices have to be true to who I am. You've coaxed me out of my comfort zone. You've helped me grow into a slightly more adventurous version of myself. But I'm still me. I still like to be in control and organized and punctual. And with or without you, I'm ready to embrace my life.

MARSDEN (hugs her): I'm so proud of you. And there's always the chance we'll meet again.

AVA (smiles): And if we do, I'll definitely show you my feet.

After the Author releases us, Ava and I shuffle over to the craft table, but the pickings are slim: a few puckered cherry tomatoes and sweating cheese cubes.

"This is where we met," Ava says. "It wasn't even that long ago, but I feel like I've known you forever."

With her disheveled hair and sloppy sweatshirt, she's never looked more endearing. I'm going to miss her. I tell her so.

She nods. "This is the last time I'm going to see you, isn't it?"

"Probably. I'm guessing that was my last scene."

"Sure seemed like it." She pokes at a cube of cheese.

"I mean, you'll see Marsden again. A lot."

"But Marsden isn't you."

It's such an affirmation to hear her say that. "No, he's not."

"You know, the Author has already written the ending."

I'm slightly taken aback. Though the Author jumped around with her kissing scenes, she wrote mostly in a linear fashion. "So what happens?"

"You'll have to read the book," Ava teases.

"You're hilarious."

"Okay, fine. I'll tell you. After Marsden leaves, Rafferty tries to win Ava back, but she refuses him. The book ends with Ava choosing #TeamAva." She pumps her fist up and down. "Girl power!"

"Wow. Props to the Author for making such a bold choice. Are you happy with it?"

She smiles. "You know what? I am. Ava has her whole life ahead of her. She'll have so many more chances for love and connection."

It's weird to hear Ava talk about herself in the third person, but I guess that means she's come to terms with the paradox of being a fictional character. "I wish you both the very best." I give her a hug that lingers.

"Good luck with your hearing. I'll be rooting for you."

Neither of us wants to say goodbye. So we don't. She kisses me on the cheek and watches me wistfully as I push my button to return home.

CHAPTER 45

Zelda picks me up again for un-therapy, and we spend the walk alternating between flirting adorably and plotting ways to get to George.

"I bet Finn would be good at this," I say wistfully. "Clearly he was much better at subterfuge than I realized."

Zelda puts a consoling arm around me. "Hey, if you're still bothered that he told me certain things he never told you . . . for what it's worth, I think he was trying to protect you. He didn't want to give you incomplete information that you might act on impulsively."

"I'm no more impulsive than any other Manic Pixie," I protest.

"There's a difference between crafting the appearance of reckless abandon and actually committing to harebrained schemes. Just because I playfully wear unmatched socks doesn't mean I'm going to go cliff-diving in a thunderstorm."

I don't know how to respond to that, so instead I tell Zelda about Nebraska's hatbox room, and she offers to help me get a look at Finn's letter. None of this is getting us closer to freeing George, but maybe once I get some answers about Finn my brain will have more room to focus on rescue plans.

When we arrive at Nebraska's house, I immediately begin to mainline coffee and make sure Nebraska notices. I'll need another bathroom break, and when I go, Finn's letter will be mine.

Morale among our group has hit an all-time low. I never imagined we could be so worried and sad that we'd lose our Manic. This might be totally unprecedented for our Trope.

Angela encourages us to meditate for the first portion of our session. She leads us through deep breathing exercises, but she can't keep her focus, and she continually loses the count. I've never seen her frazzled like this.

Finally she gives up and lets us manage our own breathing. I try my best to relax, but I can't get into it. George's empty chair seems to mock me. I imagine I can see a face in the wrought iron fleur-de-lis. The eyes bore into me, challenging me to find a way to save my friend. I can't stand to look at it anymore, and the whole luxurious formality of Nebraska's veranda bears down oppressively.

"Can we do this somewhere else?" I feel a rush of temporary relief for breaking the silence.

Angela startles at my harshness. "Like where? Out on the lawn?"

Since the lawn witnessed the scene of Nebraska and George's last showdown, we need somewhere fresh.

"How about the ballroom?" Nebraska suggests. She certainly has a knack for picking up on my vibe.

"That's such an awesome idea, Nebraska," Sky exclaims, a little overeager in her campaign to win Nebraska's favor. Sky kicks Chloe's leg under the table, from an angle Nebraska can't possibly see.

"Uh . . . I'd rather stay here." Chloe tries to make up some sort of dissent on the fly. "The ballroom is so drafty and . . . musty."

"Overruled!" Sky shouts gleefully, launching out of her chair and spinning her way toward the ballroom. She doesn't even seem to notice that her headphones fly off on the way. "C'mon everyone!"

While the rest of us are uncharacteristically sluggish, Sky and Nebraska hoot and boot-scoot in figure eights below the chandelier, as if they're worshipping an idol.

Meanwhile Angela, apparently drained of her will to lead, slumps against the far wall. I plop down in the middle of the floor and nurse my coffee. Zelda hunkers down next to me, close enough that our thighs touch. Mandy and Chloe sit facing us, so that we form a loose circle.

Sky approaches, breathlessly, and starts going around our circle and tapping our heads.

"Duck," she says to me.

"Duck," she says to Zelda.

"Duck," she says to Mandy.

"GOOSE!" she shouts over Chloe and starts running in a zig-zag pattern. When faced with such tempting silliness, Chloe can't really help herself, and she chases Sky down until she manages to tackle her.

"Oooof!" Sky exclaims as she hits the floor. "You don't need to be so rough, just because you're all upset. Geez."

"You should have more respect for George," Chloe admonishes. She gets up and stalks back over to our circle.

Nebraska grins and offers Sky a hand. "Are you okay? Chloe sure is endearingly clumsy and indelicate, isn't she?"

The rest of us exchange glances. The trap is set.

But we don't have much time to take satisfaction in our deviousness, because Bridget appears between the French doors of the ballroom.

"What an unusual unofficial session this is, Angela," she trills. "Un-therapy, do you call it?"

Angela sits up straighter, more like her usual self. "Different Tropes respond to different methods."

"I would have expected to find these Manic Pixies preparing their defense," Bridget says. "After all, the hearing is the day after tomorrow."

Like we needed the reminder that our time is running low. "We'll be ready," I declare in a tone that is light-years more confident than I actually am.

Bridget adjusts the collar of her severe black suit jacket and wrinkles her nose. "In any case, I am here to fetch Angela."

Angela scrambles to stand up. "What's this all about?"

"You are in contempt of the Council by neglecting to appear for work reassignment. I'm here to escort you to the employment office, since you cannot seem to find it on your own."

"Before I go, I want to leave you all with some words of comfort and inspiration." Angela begins to walk toward our circle, but Bridget stops her.

"No time for such drivel, Angela."

Angela sighs and follows Bridget out of the ballroom. But when she reaches the doors, she turns and shouts, "Remember you are awesome!"

The chandelier continues to shake long after she's gone.

CHAPTER 46

My fellow Manic Pixies lie around in various states of distress after this latest blow.

I, on the other hand, am on high alert. As upset as I am about losing Angela, I recognize this as a perfect opportunity to set off on my mission. If Nebraska remains distracted, then maybe I won't get caught.

I whisper my intentions to Zelda.

She nods. "I'm going with you. We're in this together."

We thread through Nebraska's labyrinth of a house along the same route I used last time, via the veranda and kitchen. I count off the doors in the long hallway until we reach the hatbox room.

I head straight to the shelf where I saw Finn's letter and prop a ladder against the wall beside it. Zelda holds it while I climb, perhaps hoping to avert the same sort of disaster we caused in the glass factory. I grab hold of the letter, my hands shaking.

Finn's handwriting slants forward like it's in as much of a hurry to get somewhere as he was. His voice and his throaty laugh and the way he'd scrunch up his face and rock out all come flooding back, and I'm so overcome by his absence, I can't move. I wish I could call time-out on the universe and give him a moment of respectful silence, but I will myself to move.

I descend a few rungs so that Zelda can peek over my shoulder and read with me.

Dearest Nebs,

I've been lying here staring at all the glitter you smeared on my ceiling and thinking about how you told me that the stars are within my grasp, if I only dare to seek them.

You're a gift that I never knew I needed. Beneath your layer of pretty wrapping paper, you're a box of endless inspiration and delight. I'd milk this metaphor for miles, but I'm sure you'd remind me that I tend to get carried away when it comes to you.

But who could blame me? Not the Council. Not all my Authors. Not anyone in Reader World. You're not just a dream girl, you're my dream girl.

I won't divulge our plan to Riley, because I know you said it's safer for you and other Legacies this way—even though I would certainly trust him not to turn you in to the Council. Before you follow me on the train to our future together, would you do me the favor of delivering the enclosed letter to him? He's my best friend, and I want him to be able to make the same informed decision about his life that you allowed me to make by disclosing the secret of where the train really goes.

See you soon—I'll be waiting at the other end of the line every afternoon until you join me.

Yours forever,
Finn

"Wow," Zelda says. "This is insane! We could blackmail her with this and get her to take us to George."

"You're right." Nebraska told Finn that the Termination Train would take him somewhere other than oblivion. If she was telling the truth, she divulged classified information to a non-Legacy. If she lied, then she sent Finn to his death. In either case, she'd face punishment if the Council found out. The letter Finn enclosed for me is long gone—likely Nebraska really did burn that—but her letter alone is enough for our purposes.

My pulse racing, I tuck the letter into my pocket.

I grab Zelda's hand and turn to go, but Nebraska blocks our escape route. Her lips smile, but her eyes glint with steel so sharp, they could cut both of us in half.

"Well, well," she says. "Look at the two little lovebirds, lurking around. Didn't I warn you to be more careful?"

CHAPTER 47

Instinct opens my mouth to scream, though I don't know what purpose it would serve. The others have probably left already, and Nebraska wouldn't outright murder us in her own home. Even a Legacy wouldn't get away with that.

Zelda squeezes my hand so tightly, I think she may break it.

Nebraska must sense our agitation, because she shushes me. "Don't be *afraid* of me, dears. We're on the same side."

"Are we?" What I read makes me wary, and I haven't even fully processed it yet.

"Of course. You found Finn's letter, didn't you?"

"Yes," I admit. "But the letter suggests we're *not* on the same side."

"Riley, dear, who alerted you to the existence of the letter in the first place? And who kept it around for you to find?"

The answer to both of these questions is Nebraska. "But why not just give me the letter or deliver Finn's letter to me like he asked you to?"

"I know you must have lots and lots of questions, and I appreciate that. I enjoy intellectual curiosity and figuring out puzzles and going on adventures."

"Yet I notice you didn't end up going on the adventure

you planned with Finn," I say, hoping she doesn't notice where I've hidden the letter and trying to keep my voice calm. "Even after you went against Council regulations to share classified information with him—information that only a Legacy is supposed to know."

This is merely an educated guess on my part, but Nebraska juts out her jaw. "My intentions have always been noble." She obviously feels justified, and she refuses to apologize for anything.

I shouldn't aggravate her if I want a confession. Not that I can necessarily believe what she has to tell me, but I know that even lies hold a kernel of truth, and that's a start at least. So I look her straight in the eye. "Okay, Nebraska. We're listening."

She averts her gaze to my neck and shoulder region. "Neither of you were here to experience our golden age. We had the respect of our fellow Tropes. Readers adored us—they sent fan mail by the boatload."

"We saw." Zelda gestures at the shelves.

"None of these letters are recent," Nebraska complains.

I tap my foot. I'm antsy to move forward with our plan, but first I need some answers. "So Finn . . ." I prompt.

"The fan letters stopped coming about the same time that Finn appeared." Nebraska fluffs her hair. "It's only logical to see a connection there."

Zelda stares at Nebraska incredulously. "You resented Finn because you thought he was the reason you stopped getting *fan mail*?"

Nebraska hooks her fingers through a rung of the ladder like she might be preparing to climb. "Finn was an anomaly. Manic Pixies are Dream *Girls* and then here came this boy. He was a threat to our kind, you understand."

Oh, I understand, all right. And I'm furious. "So you had to get rid of him."

She doesn't even have the decency to deny it. "He fell in love with me easily enough . . ."

"But you had to break up with Angela to fully convince him of your plan."

Nebraska shrugs. "Collateral damage."

"And then you convinced him to board the Termination Train. But where did it take him?"

"C'mon, Riley. You're smart enough to have put this together by now. What destination could possibly convince Finn to risk everything?"

Of course I know, and I finally understand why Finn went. He'd rather take a leap of faith than continue to live in the shadow of others' expectations. "Reader World."

She claps. Slowly. Perhaps a bit sarcastically.

"So the train really leads to Reader World?" My heart blows hope bubbles in my chest.

"Yes."

CHAPTER 48

Reader World is a magical place. You know this, because you live there. Every day is like living in a choose-your-own-adventure novel. Do you even realize how lucky you are?

CHAPTER 49

"And you know that for a fact, do you?" Zelda spits out. "Or maybe you're just saying you know because it sounds better than admitting you basically tricked someone into killing himself. You make me sick." She's shaking with righteous anger and looks like she might resort to physical violence.

"Zelda!" I put a placating hand on her arm. Attacking our Trope's most ardent defender doesn't seem like a sound strategic move, especially if we still want to use her to get to George. "Maybe we should give Nebraska the benefit of the doubt."

But Zelda pulls roughly out of my grasp. "No, Riley. There's no doubt here. Nebraska is a liar and murderer."

Nebraska smirks like she's actually enjoying Zelda's outburst. "You have such an active imagination, dear. I've always appreciated that about you."

Zelda visibly deflates. She must realize that no amount of censure will penetrate Nebraska's sunny veneer of denial. It's simply not worth it to engage her.

With Zelda neutralized, Nebraska fixes her attention back on me. "You believe me, don't you?"

"I don't know," I admit. "But I do know that a Legacy could get in a lot of trouble if the Council found out she had told a regular Trope about this. We're willing to keep this information to ourselves—instead of reporting you—if you'll get us into the Villain Zone to see George. Right, Zelda?"

"Unlike you," Zelda says evenly, "we aren't backstabbers, so we'll actually keep our word."

Nebraska shrugs off this insult and considers us for a moment. "Since you seem determined to see George, I'll take you. But it's not because I feel threatened by you. You still need me."

"But only until after the Pixie-Off," I remind her.

"Fair enough," she concedes. Her viselike fingers clamp down both on my forearm and Zelda's wrist. She pulls us apart. "Let's go right now, then."

Nebraska leads us down the hallway toward the front of the house. After a few twists and turns we emerge in her foyer. Nebraska stops to retrieve an intricately woven shawl from a coat closet, and we continue on our way.

She flags down a bicycle taxi at the guard station and directs the driver to the southern gate. At first, the driver refuses to take all three of us, but Nebraska insists we'll assume all liability for overfilling the cab. Zelda sits on my lap, which I'd enjoy more under less stressful circumstances.

I'm still thinking about our conversation in the hatbox room. It's completely plausible that as a Legacy, Nebraska has been entrusted with details of how to get to Reader World. Finn might still be alive. The possibility of seeing my friend again is so tantalizing that I can barely focus on how we are going to pull off actually rescuing George once we get to the VZ.

"If the Termination Train really leads to Reader World," I address Nebraska, "why didn't you take it too?"

Nebraska sighs. "The truth is, Reader World scares me,

and it should scare you, too. What makes you think a Trope could even survive living in a complex, undirected environment like that? We aren't built for it."

"I'd like to think we could rise to the challenge," I say. "Haven't you always wanted to live life on your own terms?"

"Sure I have, Riley. But I'm being pragmatic. In Trope-Town, everything is taken care of for us. Out there in Reader World, we'd have to fend for ourselves. Are you willing to endure hardship and hunger and *aging* just to be able to make all your own decisions? I'm not."

I don't reply because Nebraska has a point. As fictional characters, we do come with our own set of advantages. While I personally don't think these advantages outweigh the right to self-determination, I'm willing to concede the view looks different from a Legacy perch. After all, Nebraska has a lot more to give up than I do.

Our journey reverses the one I took with Angela, up until we hit the Administration District. South of that, we enter the Wrong Side of the Tracks.

The buildings here press and lean against one another as though they might collapse given a gusty wind. Many of them appear abandoned or condemned, boarded up and sprouting mold. Threadbare towels and stained garments hang from sagging windows. The air stinks of decay and curdled milk.

Why does the Council waste their time on trying to eliminate our comparatively innocuous Trope when far more pressing issues abound?

Beggars lift their bowls half-heartedly as we breeze by, and that same troop of Plucky Street Urchins chases us down, still trying to offload their roses. Nebraska tosses a few coins at the Urchins, and they blow kisses and sing a song of gratitude.

"They're adorable, aren't they?" she says. "I want to pinch their chubby cheeks."

"Yeah, except you'd get your hands dirty." My comment is sardonic, but Nebraska doesn't take it that way.

"Which is exactly why I keep my distance."

Finally, we reach the Great Southern Wall. I've never been to visit in person. It's so high, I crimp my neck looking up at the barbed wire that lines the top.

Our driver stops in front of the iron gate. "I don't go any farther than this, miss."

"I'm aware of that. Thank you." Nebraska draws her shawl tighter around her shoulders, perhaps to ward off the chill in her voice. "Wait here for us."

He doesn't answer until we disembark, but as soon as we're clear, he says "Sorry, miss," and peddles back north.

Nebraska merely sighs as if she expected nothing less. "Well, then. Welcome to the Villain Zone."

CHAPTER 50

At the gate, Nebraska hands her Legacy ID to the Surly Security Guards and announces that we're her guests. The guards subject us to an invasive pat-down. They even make us take off our shoes, and they wave a metal detector wand over us.

We don't carry any bags, but they search our pockets. They ignore Finn's letter in my pocket but pull out a silver flask from the oversized right front pocket of Nebraska's butterfly-printed romper.

"No liquids over 100 milliliters in the VZ," a guard says, shaking the flask so that its contents slosh within. "You'll have to dispose of it if you want to enter."

Nebraska liberates her flask, twists open the cap, and downs her libation in one continuous swallow.

She probably has the tolerance of a team of oxen, so I don't worry that she'll cause a drunken scene. A Manic Pixie scene, maybe, but those are so delightful.

At least we don't have to wait in a ginormous line. We're the only people requesting entry, and the approximately forty-seven guards look extremely bored.

Customs officials issue us VZ visitor passes with our names and Trope designations to wear on lanyards around our necks.

Because she's Legacy, Nebraska gets a gold rope lanyard while Zelda and I have to slum it with standard-issue white string.

Once we clear the screening process, a guard leads us to the visitor's walkway. The enclosed steel catwalk loops around the inside of the wall with an intricate system of ladders that leads down to ground level and up to guard towers. From this vantage point, we have a bird's-eye view of the entire Villain Zone, which, aside from its preponderance of bunkers, appears to be a fairly normal town.

"Your pass unlocks any gate to which you have access," the guard explains. He's young and tough with a buzz cut and an angry pink scar across his neck. Excellent grammar though.

"I know my way around," Nebraska says by way of dismissal. He salutes her and retreats back into the guard station.

As we walk, Nebraska points out various villainous landmarks—the Bounty Hunter Bar, the High-Roller Casino, the Inn of No Return, and the Wax Museum Morgue.

I shiver. We don't need to extend our sightseeing to include any of those venues. "Where's the jail?" I ask Nebraska.

"All in good time. First there's something else I want to show you."

I'd like to demand that she take us directly to George, but Zelda and I are pretty much at Nebraska's mercy. Maybe this blackmail plan wasn't as clever as we thought it was.

Finally, she unlocks the sixth gate we come to (yes, I'm counting—in case we need to make a quick escape), and we take the ladder down, Nebraska ahead of us. When we get to the bottom, Nebraska turns and knocks on the door.

Zelda takes advantage of this distraction to mouth, "What is happening?"

I shake my head to indicate I have no idea.

A tall man in a linen suit and Panama hat opens up and flashes us a genuine smile. "Welcome to the Trope Museum," he says in a vaguely European accent. "I am Milton, and I will be your guide today."

Purely on the basis of where he works, I know he has to be some sort of criminal type, and judging from his dapper style and cultured bearing, I'm going to guess Art Thief or Con Man.

He retrieves a pair of horn-rimmed reading glasses from his shirt pocket and examines our passes. "Ah, Manic Pixies. Your visit cannot be a coincidence."

"Whatever do you mean?" Nebraska asks.

"If I followed the rules, I would not tell you. But luckily for you three, I have anarchist tendencies." He twirls his mustache. "The Council sent a memo about you. The Trope Museum is preparing your exhibit—the final resting place for the Manic Pixie Dream Girl Trope."

CHAPTER 51

"But we're not dead yet," Nebraska protests, looking genuinely shocked now. "We still have our hearing, and I'm confident we will prevail. Or, at least I will." Classic Nebraska. But I'm so shaken, I can only summon the briefest flash of outrage at her selfishness.

"I do hope so, milady." Milton tips his hat. "Your Trope enchants me. It would be a shame to have you all flattened to microfilm."

A tremor runs through me. I try to imagine what it feels like to no longer exist—if it'll just be nothingness or, more frightening still, if my awareness of myself will still be there but without form or function.

"It's not fair," I protest. My chest tightens. The low ceiling seems to press down on me.

Milton chuckles. "Life is not fair. Do you expect fiction to be any different?"

"Shouldn't fiction satisfy at least?" I ask. "Like, shouldn't the Reader turn the last page with a feeling of triumph over incredible odds?"

"Ah, it is refreshing to encounter an idealist in these parts. I, too, was once a true believer in the Happily Ever After."

I don't know if I should take this as a compliment, considering the source. "And then what happened?"

"The Council lent me out to too many hack writers who did so little research and had so little grasp of the art of nuance that they twisted me into a string of terrible stereotypes, each time ripping out a piece of my soul. Finally, I begged to be transferred, and now I work here, which is perhaps even more depressing as I am confronted daily by Authorial abuses of Tropes." He waves his arm, beckoning us to follow. "Which is a perfect segue into my tour."

We stand in front of a dim alcove containing several dark-skinned mannequins dressed in ill-fitting clothing. The pant legs, collars, and suit sleeves are all too short, too long, or too baggy.

A steel arch frames the exhibit. It turns out to be a micro-film storage system made up of dozens of drawers. Milton picks one seemingly at random, pulls it out, and rifles through the plastic cases until he comes to one labeled *Jerome*.

I come to understand that these drawers contain hundreds or even thousands of individuals from a discontinued Trope. Each one had hopes and dreams cruelly cut short. Each one once had the freedom to walk the streets of TropeTown.

They were once like me, and I may soon be like them.

Milton loads Jerome into a projector. His image bursts onto the wall. I have to look away, and Zelda flinches beside me. Jerome crosses his eyes, sticks out his tongue and wears a clown hat. "Can any of you tell me which Trope Jerome is?"

"I'd guess Uncle Tomfoolery," Nebraska says, only slightly less aghast than I feel.

"Exactly." Milton turns off the projector. "Authors used him as comic relief and to make the other characters seem competent in comparison. The Trope is no longer sanctioned due to racism."

"Because the other characters were white," Nebraska states.

"Actually, it's because the Uncle Tomfoolery Tropes comprise the most offensive stereotypical slanders of black men handed down from the time of slavery in Reader World. Authors portrayed them as superstitious, easily frightened, incompetent, and worse."

We slide over to the next alcove. More mannequins. More drawers. More dreams forever suspended in time.

Milton selects a plastic case labeled *Porter* and loads him into the projector.

"Porter exemplifies the outdated and offensive Magical Negro Trope," Milton explains. "His purpose was to show the protagonist how to save the day or provide an awakening of some sort. This Trope also lost its sanction due to racism, despite embodying positive characteristics such as wisdom, patience, and selflessness."

"Because the other characters were white," Nebraska states for the second time, but this time she seems less sure of herself.

"The protagonist was almost universally white," Milton confirms. "Which is indeed problematic, but there's much more to it. As white Readers and Authors have become more socially and culturally aware, demand has grown for diverse characters to be portrayed sensitively and authentically. This means Authors strive to create more Developeds instead of relying so heavily on Tropes."

Nebraska harrumphs. "What these *enlightened* Readers seem to be missing is that not all characters can be developed in a story. It would weigh down the narrative. Tropes exist for a good reason."

I'm not surprised to hear her say this. As a Legacy, Nebraska benefits from the status quo. Of course she doesn't welcome social progress with open jazz hands.

"While that's true," Milton says, "if we don't get a range of diverse Developed characters, all Readers ever see are minorities reduced to a very specific set of qualities that then become ingrained stereotypes."

Zelda shifts her weight from leg to leg, looking like she might be prepping to run. "So what you're saying is that a Magical Negro is not a person so much as a very narrow idea of a person."

Milton beams at her. "Right. And that's dehumanizing and objectifying."

"It seems to me that most Tropes are not inherently offensive," I say, thinking of my own Trope and all the wonderful friends I've made within it at group therapy. "It's how Authors use them. Like what if all the characters had been minorities? That would be less racist, would it?"

Milton winks at me. "Much like if a Manic Pixie exists in a novel full of other Manic Pixies, it is less sexist."

"Exactly! Doesn't the Council consider that?"

"I have no idea what the Council considers in their deliberations," Milton says, "but what you're getting at is Trope subversion. That's when an Author takes a familiar Trope and does something unusual with it. So instead of Readers' expectations being fulfilled, Readers are forced to confront the fact that people really are more complex than our labels give them credit for. Unfortunately, Authors don't rise to this challenge remotely as often as they should."

I seethe with the unjustness of it all. The Council punished Jerome and Porter and all the others for something they had no control over. Instead of retiring them, the Council could have set them free in Reader World, where they could've grown beyond the flaws in their programming, making their own choices and living for themselves.

I bet the offending Authors never paid any penance for their insensitivity.

I'm hit with a horrifying realization—what if my very existence as a Trope gives Authors an excuse to be lazy and propagate negative, objectifying portrayals? Maybe I *am* toxic despite my best intentions.

"The Manic Pixie Trope is in the same subset of Tropes as the Magical Negro." Milton urges us onwards. "You are all considered Magical Secondary Characters. There is the Magical Asian . . ." At the next alcove, he gives us a quick glimpse of an older man with a white beard in martial arts attire.

"And the Magical Shaman . . ." We wander over to the next alcove for a brief look at a man in a feathered headdress.

"Magical Secondary Characters suffer from being cast in supporting roles instead of as the heroes of their own stories. But the worst part is that they often sacrifice themselves for the benefit of the white male protagonist, which sends the harmful message that the white male is somehow more worthy of survival."

"You're a white male," Nebraska points out to Milton. "Why do you care?"

He blushes and stammers. "It's my job."

Nebraska clicks her tongue in judgment. "Are you saying you wouldn't care otherwise?"

"I'd probably still be ignorant," Milton admits. "Now I'm aware of my privilege. I know I don't have all the answers, but I'm committed to learning and supporting the discussion."

"Such a virtuous villain you are," Nebraska quips.

His improved posture indicates he doesn't catch the undercurrent of contempt in her voice. "There are three other

Magical Minority Tropes in addition to yours under consideration for the chopping block." He pulls a few photos from his pocket and shows them to us.

". . . the Gay Best Friend . . ." The photo here depicts a young man wearing fur legwarmers and a crisp white shirt unbuttoned nearly to the waist.

". . . the cancer patient child . . ." A little bald girl with enormous eyes in a hospital setting with tubes everywhere.

". . . and the Rainman." A childlike man wearing a sailor suit, who seems to be controlling the floating objects surrounding him.

"But those categories are so broad!" Zelda exclaims. "I mean, every gay person must be someone's best friend, right?"

Milton returns the photos to his pocket. "Admit it—when I say 'Gay Best Friend,' a very specific picture comes to mind—much like the one I just showed you. You know this guy from so many stories, and he's always the same. He's flamboyant and funny. He gives his gal pals great dating advice and loves to help them pick out flattering clothes. But does he ever get a date of his own? Do his gal pals pick out clothes for him? Not bloody often. A magical Secondary Character shouldn't be seen as anyone's servant. They should get some tangible benefits from the protagonist, don't you think?"

"Ummm . . ." Nebraska says. "I think you're preaching to the choir. We have this same problem in the Manic Pixie Trope."

Milton clears his throat. "Which brings me to our last exhibit today . . ."

We round the corner. The Manic Pixie alcove is nearly finished.

It's even worse than we thought. They've already begun the process of condemning us to this dusty place.

CHAPTER 52

The mannequins lean against the walls, already half-dressed. One of them looks just like me, down to wearing the yellow baseball cleats I scuffed on the ice while doing snow angels with Zelda at Winter Lake.

Clearly they mean to make an example of me. They want to show how my choice of fanciful footwear somehow contributed to the downfall of an entire Trope.

"Oh my god, that's supposed to be Riley!" Zelda says in a choked voice. She's shaking, and her expression vacillates between outrage and abject terror.

I nod because my throat is a desert, and I'm too afraid to speak. The Council could be judging us right now, spying on us via hidden cameras, ready to use anything we say to defend ourselves as more proof that we're toxic.

"I can't believe this." Nebraska levies a series of harsh curses before clamping a hand over her own mouth. She composes herself and glares at Milton. "What vicious falsehoods have tainted our good name?"

"Well," Milton says carefully, "some in Reader World say you are one-dimensional characters with no inner life or goals of your own."

Nebraska lets out a laugh so harsh it could rip someone's throat out. Possibly Milton's. "Manic Pixies are beautifully multifaceted, well-rounded, and deep. Whoever thinks otherwise hasn't experienced the pleasure of getting to know me."

"You mean us," Zelda corrects.

"Us," Nebraska repeats, but in an unconvincingly smarmy way.

I try to see the issue from the Reader World perspective. My Author gave Marsden goals that had nothing to do with Ava. But I've also been part of projects where my role was far less nuanced, as we all have. We complained about it enough in therapy sessions.

"What else?" Nebraska demands.

"It's sexist," Milton says.

"Nonsense!" Her eyes land on me and narrow. "We have Riley to prove otherwise."

Am I the token boy though? One exception to the rule doesn't necessarily let our trope off the hook for its historic objectification of women.

I understand now why some people in Reader World would want us to be retired. And maybe it *would* be for the best if Authors stopped leaning so heavily on our Trope. But do I deserve to be locked away forever, far from public consumption, because of what I am and what I represent?

Does Zelda? Or Nebraska, or any of the others?

We're not just reductive stereotypes. We're so much more than that. Or if we're not, we *can* be.

Milton shrugs, clearly not invested enough to make a counter-argument. "Also, some say the term itself is restrictive, because it lumps all 'quirky' women together, essentially dismissing them."

Nebraska ponders this for a moment as if it stumps her. She pulls out her flask and tries to take a sip, apparently forgetting that the guards emptied it. She shakes it sadly and returns it to her pocket. Finally she squares her shoulders. "Well, you know what? I embrace the term. I'm a Manic Pixie Dream Girl, and I'm damn proud of it. And why shouldn't I be? Don't you agree, Riley?"

Honestly, after everything Nebraska's done, if the Council said they were going to lock only Nebraska in this exhibit and let the rest of us go free, maybe I'd be okay with it. But the way things stand, we need her if the rest of us are going to survive.

And we deserve to survive.

"Yes," I say. "We should all be proud of who we are. Manic Pixies are awesome. And we're going to prove it to the Council . . . and to the world."

CHAPTER 53

"Thank you for the tour, Milton," Nebraska says ever so politely. "I think we've seen quite enough."

We've seen more than enough, but we still need to free George. Now that we're more determined than ever to fight the Council, saving George is my top priority. Would Milton be willing to help Zelda and me instigate a jailbreak?

"The Council detained one of our fellow Manic Pixies here in the VZ," I say casually, brushing off some imaginary dust from my shoulder. "Have you seen her?"

"I have not," he says. "But I hear she is quite the spit*fire*—in more ways than one."

"Oh, Milton! You rascal!" Nebraska's giggles bubble over us, making me cringe.

He leads us back to the entrance. Milton shakes my hand and pats Zelda on the back. He kisses both Nebraska's cheeks in the European way.

"Good luck," he says. "Perhaps I will see you again, perhaps I will not."

Nebraska, Zelda, and I climb the ladder back to the catwalk.

"Milton seems nice," Zelda remarks. "Other than terrifying us with portents of our imminent demise."

We edge closer to the fence. I scan all the buildings, wondering which might be the jail that currently houses George.

"People generally expect Villainous Tropes to be these awful brutes every second of every day," Nebraska says. "But when they aren't performing their dastardly deeds, they default to friendly. It makes them even scarier, if you ask me."

Did she ever consider that Milton might actually be a good person? Maybe even kindhearted enough to help us escape our fate, if he had the chance? I need to pump Nebraska for information—anything that might help to keep us all from our proposed microfilm prison.

"So why did you bring us here?" I ask.

"I wanted you to have the context to see the bigger picture." She swings her arms out to show how big this picture should be. "I thought if you had context, you might not judge me so harshly for all the things I've done in the name of preserving our Trope's livelihood."

Zelda scoffs. "Like framing George for arson and murdering Finn—"

"I did not murder Finn," Nebraska snaps. "In fact, turns out I did him a favor by sending him to Reader World. Now he won't have to share in our Trope's demise."

A tremor runs through me. "What are you saying? You think we'll lose our appeal to the Council?"

Nebraska grimaces. It's not a good look for her, or one that seems particularly at home on her face. "I'll be real with you, because you deserve that. If the Council has gone so far as to start our exhibit, then this Trope is pretty much screwed."

"So what about that rousing speech you gave Milton back there?" Zelda asks.

"Hey, a Legacy Manic Pixie Dream Girl has to hold out at

least a glimmer of hope to keep up appearances." She holds up invisible pom-poms. "Rah, rah, rah. Go team!"

"You don't even know what a team is," Zelda states, echoing my thoughts.

"Speaking of which," Nebraska says, like something mind-blowing just occurred to her, "our *team* should not include Manic Pixie Dream Boys. Society didn't turn against us until your kind came along. All this unrest is *your* fault, and I will not have you ruining our defense, too."

Panic eats at the lining of my stomach. "No," I protest weakly.

Nebraska steps in close and pats me down until she finds Finn's letter and pulls it out of my pocket. "Can't let you keep this, sorry."

She throws a pitying look to Zelda. "I hope you understand that I never intended for you to be caught up in this. But they do say you should be careful of the company you keep, so I guess I can't feel that sorry for you." She extracts a plastic whistle from her bra and blows on it.

"What are you talking about?" My hands start to tremble so I shove them in my now empty pockets.

The guard with the pink neck scar approaches.

"I know you two wanted to visit George," Nebraska says sweetly. "So I arranged this guard to take you to her holding cell."

I look from her to the guard and back, my heart hemorrhaging fear.

"Wait!" Zelda lunges for Nebraska, but the guard steps between them and physically restrains her. "You can't do this!"

"I'm merely doing what you asked me to do. Tell George I send my greetings." Nebraska gives us a half-wave and swishes off in her silks.

CHAPTER 54

The guard blindfolds us and leads us semi-roughly around the catwalk. I quickly get disoriented and have no idea where we are by the time he finally forces us down a ladder. So much for counting our steps and finding my way back.

The guard's keys jangle against metal, and a door scrapes open. The air feels thicker. At first, I can't hear anything but Zelda's heavy, fast breathing and our shoes hitting the concrete under us. But soon a single plinking sound multiplies into a cacophony of chaos.

"Settle down," the guard commands, and the noise stops immediately. He rips the blindfold from my eyes, and I blink several times to get my bearings.

We're in a cellblock, for sure, with bars and bunks and assorted prisoners in orange jumpsuits holding up spoons, but all the sliding cell doors are open.

The guard pushes us over to one of the cells. George sits at a desk, making notations on a pad of paper with a purple fountain pen. She has modified her jumpsuit into a halter and skirt combo, with a strip of the ripped fabric holding back her hair.

"Welcome to jail," the guard says. He taps his guard stick

on George's desk, and she finally glances up and notices us.

"Riley! Zelda! How fabulous to see you!" She launches herself at us for a group reunion hug.

"No touching!" the guard admonishes, and the hug ends as quickly as it began. He takes his leave without giving us any further instructions or information. So unsettling.

"Are they treating you okay?" Zelda scans our friend's body for any signs of abuse or neglect, but truth be told, George's skin glows like she's been at a spa rather than in jail.

George grins. "Everyone is so nice. Most of them are Prisoner and Guard Tropes, so Authors have them work a lot, but when they're around, we have the best time. Right now, I'm teaching them to tap dance."

I trace the unused lock on her cell door. "So, they don't lock you in?"

"Only the outside door," George says.

"We need to escape." I give her a condensed version of what has happened since the Council carted her off, and her face grows more alarmed by the sentence.

"Nebraska is such an idiot," George says to me. "You're not the destroyer of our Trope, you're going to be the one who saves it. Instead of trying to get rid of you, she needs to parade you in front of the Council."

"What do you mean?" I ask.

"Our Trope is sexist because it's 99.9 percent females in quirky muse roles. That makes it all too easy for society to dismiss the Manic Pixie as a girl thing, like menstrual cramps and the birth control pill."

Zelda catches George's drift. "But if we had more male representation, then we'd be taken more seriously. You're a genius, George!"

"Why thank you." George flaps her notebook in the air. "I also have a plan to break out of jail. That's what I've been working on. And with you two here, the chances of success have improved markedly."

"Even if we get out of this building, how are we going to get out of the VZ?" Zelda literally wrings her hands. "There's a giant wall and tons of guards."

"I have that covered, too," George says. "No worries."

Jail time has given George an insane amount of focus, and I tell her as much.

"It's given me time to think about what's really important and put Angela's self-care strategies into practice," she says. "All my conflict with Nebraska has been distracting me from working on my own issues. It's up to me to improve my own attitudes, regardless of external circumstances."

George is a lot more developed and complex than she lets on. No wonder the Council considered her for Legacy status. "Why did you never tell us about being up for promotion to Legacy?" I ask.

At this, George stabs a page of her notebook with the pen, spilling purple ink everywhere. "They wanted me to deny who I am."

"How?" Zelda reaches out to still George's hand.

"I'm not going to hide any longer," George declares. "Angela and I are in love."

Aha! Angela's listlessness after George's arrest makes sense now. "You make a great couple," I say.

George blushes. "Thank you. I wish everyone were as open-minded. The Council claimed Legacies should embody the most renowned traits of their Tropes."

Zelda takes the pen from George and adds a few defiant

stabs of her own. "And they want to put you in a heteronormative box."

"Exactly." George drops the notebook on the floor. "But I am done with boxes. And I'm done with this jail."

"Well, then, let's get this party started." I give her a twirl. "What's your plan?"

We spend the rest of the night and the next day plotting. We sleep in shifts on George's single bunk.

The morning of our Town Council defense dawns with a visit from a Mafia Maven, who introduces herself as Marla. Zelda and I rouse George from her bunk.

"Georgie, you up for another tap lesson?"

George grins. "Gather everyone you can find. Guards, too. This is going to be a routine you never forget."

Our getaway is a go, and right in the nick of time, too.

We stage an improvised jailhouse rock musical with lots of tap dancing and a rattling of the outer jailhouse keys as the central instrumental element. The Guards totally go for it, and during a furious tap-off between the svelte Mafia Maven Marla and George, I use the distraction to divest a guard of his keys, unlock the outer door, and return said keys to their owner without anyone noticing. Once everyone retires to the rec room to celebrate the Mafia Maven's tap dominance, George, Zelda, and I slip out the unlocked front door. Zelda quickly trades shirts with George, so George doesn't draw attention as a prisoner, and whoa does Zelda look good in an orange halter-top.

We climb the ladder up to the catwalk, George leading the way.

A few rungs from the top, I hear a familiar voice.

"Why, if it isn't Georgie the spitfire." Milton chuckles not at all evilly. "From the second you introduced me to the escapism of tap dance, I knew you had the ingenuity for a prison break."

"You claimed you didn't know George," I say.

"A simple ruse to keep Nebraska unaware of my deep respect for her rival," Milton explains as he gives Zelda a hand up the ladder. "When I heard about today's tap session, I got here as soon as I could, but it looks like I missed out. Come. We must hurry."

It's not super surprising that a Manic Pixie could win over a jaded villain like Milton—not to mention an entire jail population. But it's certainly a feat that George managed it within the space of a couple of days.

We don't have much choice but to trust Milton, so we do. He takes us through a chain-link door and back down a ladder that puts us onto the shadowy streets of the VZ, which is rather terrifying.

I try my best not to be distracted by Zelda's amazing abs as we follow Milton to an Abandoned Shed.

"This is as far as I go, my friends," Milton says. "Stay true to yourselves, and find ways to tell *your* stories. It is all I ask in return for my assistance today."

George throws her arms around him. "Thank you for everything. Keep practicing your shiggy bops, okay?"

"Will do." He salutes her, throws himself into a fancy tap dance step, and slips away.

We have to dig through a pile of ancient corroded saws and rakes to uncover the trap door to a tunnel that runs under the wall. Zelda flings the tools as though they're as light as plastic toys, while George stops too often to admire constellations of rust. The muscles in my arms ache with the effort, but we finally manage to move everything and lift the wood panel.

We find a flashlight taped to the underside of the trapdoor. Zelda liberates it and turns it on.

We take deep breaths and prepare to run.

Nebraska may believe I'm a liability, but with the fate of the entire Manic Pixie Trope on the line, I can't abandon my fellow Pixies. Not after all that I've witnessed here.

CHAPTER 55

The more distance we put between us and the VZ, the more we relax. We make it back to the Right Side of the Tracks with just enough time to stop by our apartments and change clothes for the Council meeting. Zelda takes George home with her to raid her wardrobe, since we suspect George's place has been cleaned out already.

I am far from looking my best. My skin is puffy from the restless sleep and tortured dreams of the past two nights. But I put on my silver sport coat and burgundy pinstripe pants borrowed once upon a time from Finn. They both suffer from wrinkles and Sprite's kitty fuzz, but they soothe me emotionally. And I need that because I am really freaking nervous. What if the Council condemns us to the Trope Museum tonight? Would they cuff us and take us away immediately? Or would I be able to jump aboard the Termination Train and take my chances there?

Town Hall sneers at us with its straight angles and cold concrete, but tonight we fight back with color. All 157 Manic Pixies have shown up in their quirky best. The Hall brims with pinafores and sashes and pink tutus. I look around the auditorium for Zelda and George but figure they're keeping a low profile.

Mandy comes up behind me and guides me into a seat in the front row. "God, Riley, did you go hamper diving?"

"Nice to see you, too," I reply. She is, of course, whimsically dressed in a flared jade vinyl dress with a cameo choker and thigh-high skin-tight jelly boots. Her lipstick blares fire-engine red. "How's Clark?"

"No idea." She lifts her palm for a high five. "Two days, no contact."

I up the ante and offer a double high five, and she goes all in for the ten. As we take our seats, I fill her in on George's safe return and Nebraska's treachery. She tells me that no one has seen Angela, but that Sky has met with Nebraska and planted the seeds of sabotage. I'm not a vindictive person by nature, but at this point, I'd relish seeing Nebraska get her comeuppance.

Nebraska struts onto the stage and stands before a clear, glass podium in a regal sleeveless jumpsuit color-blocked in jewel tones. She's honestly the only person I've ever known to pull off this style. The Council, comprised of Bridget, two other women, and one man, sits off to one side.

As Nebraska scans the crowd, her gaze falls on me. She flinches slightly in surprise, but recovers quickly with a smile that betrays begrudging admiration. She taps her chin, and I know she's plotting something, her quicksilver mind working overtime to twist my escape to her advantage.

When Bridget climbs on stage, silence fills the auditorium. She spends a moment staring down at us with her superior expression, attempting to intimidate us. Which, to be honest, works rather well, seeing as I'm trembling in my chair.

"Because she serves as a cipher whose sole purpose is to enrich and enliven the lives of depressed dudes, the Manic

Pixie Dream Girl Trope may be considered an outdated, sexist offense against humanity," Bridget says. She turns to face Nebraska. "How do you plead?"

"Thank you for your charming introduction, Bridget. It is my pleasure this evening, as the only Legacy of my illustrious Trope, to defend myself against these baseless charges."

Bridget makes her way back to the rest of the Council, who seems impressed with Nebraska's imposing stage presence. Nebraska is convincing at what she does, but her word choice, which puts the focus of her defense on herself, does not go unnoticed by the crowd. A low rumble of discontent begins to vibrate behind me.

Nebraska continues, undeterred. "Cipher characters are not inherently sexist, but rather, it is the way they are *used* that can become problematic. As you and the rest of the Council know, Bridget, Tropes aren't meant to serve the same purpose as Developeds. They don't need to be as nuanced or complex. This is, in fact, the whole guiding principle and *raison d'etre* of TropeTown. Furthermore, Manic Pixies enrich the lives of everyone they come across, not only dudes. I have a room full of letters as proof of how my dazzling personality has helped those of all gender identities in Reader World find their way through a multitude of difficult situations."

She pulls a handful of letters out of the pockets of her jumpsuit as a prop and flings them into the air. They flutter down and land squarely at my feet, a reminder of her conviction that I'm responsible for her dwindling popularity. "Just as Readers love us, so do the Developeds who headline the stories we support so selflessly. One such Developed is so enamored of our work, she broke out of her own novel to defend us here tonight."

Everyone in the room, including the awestruck Council, erupts with gasps—Developeds leaving their novels is unheard of. I get a sinking feeling at her use of feminine pronouns. Especially when Nebraska looks straight at me with a wicked grin. Has Nebraska used her Legacy status to somehow trick Ava into doing this?

Sure enough, Ava enters through a side door and climbs onstage. Her hair is pulled back in a loose ponytail and her soft pink cardigan compliments the glow in her cheeks. She looks elegant and gorgeous and determined.

I am seriously fighting tears.

Nebraska steps slightly to the side, leaving barely enough room for Ava to squeeze behind the podium. Without missing a beat, Ava hip-checks Nebraska, nudging her farther out of the spotlight. For a delightful split-second, Nebraska is thrown off-balance.

Ava sees me, and a radiant smile spreads across her face. It's so surreal to have her here in TropeTown that I grab onto the armrests of my chair for fear of floating away.

"My name is Ava Wells," she begins. "When Riley told me about the possibility of his Trope being retired, I was shocked. Riley's work as a Manic Pixie Dream Boy has depth and heart, and his positive attitude and generous spirit inspired all of us, including the Author, to see the best in ourselves. Losing Riley and those of his Trope would be a crushing blow to literature."

She pauses, fiddling with the top button of her cardigan. "And losing Riley would be a crushing blow to me."

Somebody in the audience starts clapping, and suddenly the whole room erupts in cheers.

Nebraska motions for me to join them, and Mandy pushes me up. I find my feet walking of their own accord, because I'm certainly not controlling them. I end up squeezing myself awkwardly between Ava and Nebraska.

The view from the stage overwhelms me. Over 150 sets of eyes bore into me, judging me and my rumpled appearance. I have to gulp numerous times to keep this afternoon's meager jail rations in my stomach.

"Yes, indeed." Nebraska rests a hypocritical hand on my shoulder, and it takes everything I have not to slap it away. "Riley is a noble experiment of our Trope, as was our dearly departed friend, Finn, before him. Part of what makes our Trope so great is our willingness to try out diverse sub-types, some of which are ultimately more successful than others."

I can intuit where Nebraska is going with this argument, and I need to shut her down before she lays me at the sacrificial altar to save herself.

"If it's sexism you want to combat," I interrupt, my voice shaky at first but growing steadier, "the solution is not to obliterate the Manic Pixie Dream Girl, but to level the playing field and add more Manic Pixie Dream Boys to the mix."

Nebraska's claws dig into my shoulder. She is obviously not amused, but she knows she can't risk arguing with me now.

"Riley is 100 percent correct," George calls from the audience. She leaps up from her seat at the back and runs to the stage, hopping on it and taking the mike. "Not only are we diversifying in terms of gender, but we've also become more inclusive by providing Manic Pixies of various ethnic backgrounds and sexual orientations."

George waves out into the audience. "There's Lulu, Brienne, Fatima, Aysha, Mishiko, Palak, and *me*—and dozens more who carry love and light into our literature. Reader World would be a less magical place without us. Without all of us. We don't simply enrich the lives of depressed dudes, we enrich each life we come across."

"To demonstrate this," I jump in, fired up, "several of us have collaborated with Nebraska to put together a Pixie-Off—"

Bridget pounds a wooden hammer on the table in front of her to silence us. This is the moment of truth.

"A rousing set of speeches, to be sure," Bridget says. "I'm afraid that, due to time constraints, we will have to adjourn now. However, we will reconvene tomorrow for your Pixie-Off. You are dismissed."

CHAPTER 56

A stay of execution brings collective celebratory relief, followed approximately 4.2 seconds later by individual panicky anxiety. This manifests in 150 Manic Pixies hopping, skipping, and gamboling for the exit. The remaining seven of us, stalwarts from group therapy, gather in front of the stage, joined by Ava.

No one says a thing as Bridget makes her way over to us with a quizzical expression.

Zelda gives my hand a quick squeeze, and I appreciate it. I notice she's wearing a plain white T-shirt and gold snowsuit pants with suspenders. A flashy understatement pepped up with exactly the right flair—a gold Au-79 button. The button makes me feel unreasonably hopeful about our plight.

"You certainly had some surprises up your sleeves, Nebraska," Bridget says. "Am I to understand you arranged for both Ava and Georgina to be present here today?"

"Ava and Georgina came of their own free will," Nebraska states. She's not going to confirm she's complicit in anything that could bring censure from the Council.

Bridget addresses George: "I should have my guards return you to the VZ, but frankly, I admire your spunk. You may stay on the Right Side of the Tracks at least until our final verdict tomorrow."

George and Sky exchange fist bumps, and I flash George a covert thumbs-up.

Bridget scrutinizes Ava next. "And you. You realize you cannot return to your novel, and you essentially destroyed it by leaving." The way she puts it sounds so harsh, I expect Ava to recoil.

Instead, Ava stands taller. "I had a heart-to-heart with my Author. She came to understand I had developed past the confines of the story she was writing, and she released me so I can reach my full potential. She assured me that she would continue to create, and she sends her gratitude to Riley for inspiring her to be better. She said she is proud of us, and she wishes us the best."

Bridget is rendered speechless, and I detect tears welling up in the eyes of my fellow Manic Pixies.

"That is the most beautiful thing I have ever heard," Mandy says. "You must really love Riley."

My gaze shifts from Ava to the bemused Zelda and back again. Being at the crux of a love triangle has never felt more uncomfortable.

Ava giggles. "Um, sure. I mean, I do love Riley. But I didn't come here for him."

I gulp, simultaneously relieved and puzzled. "You didn't?"

"I did this for me," she asserts. "Your belief in me made me believe in myself. I want more out of my life than cycling through the same plot over and over. I want to have adventures of my own making."

Ava partly credits her new outlook to my contribution. The sense of pride I felt the day Ava summoned me returns, and it makes me want to sweep her up into my arms.

Bridget clears her throat. "Yes, well. You will have to come with me to be processed. We can't have undocumented characters wandering around TropeTown."

"Wait . . ." I have so much I want to say to Ava. Bridget can't just drag her away.

"You should have adequate time for a reunion later," Bridget declares brusquely. But she gives Nebraska a little nod. "I must admit, your defense dazzled us today."

We're still processing this unexpected praise as she continues. "We are curious to see if you can continue to impress us with your teamwork. Come back tomorrow night at six and show us what you've got." She escorts a dazed Ava out of the room, adding over her shoulder, "But bear in mind, regardless of your individual merits or limitations, our decision will apply to the Trope as a whole."

I exchange glances with the others. It's clear we're all thinking the same thing.

To impress Bridget, we have to put our hate for Nebraska on hold.

Because if we sabotage Nebraska, we sabotage ourselves. But if we don't, we let her get away with everything.

We have a weighty decision to make.

What would Finn have us do?

Or you?

CHAPTER 57

After Bridget's pronouncement, Zelda tells me we need to talk. When did the use of that phrase ever turn out well?

Maybe she's worried that Ava's unexpected arrival in TropeTown complicates our relationship. My own feelings are so knotted, I'm not sure how reassuring I can be. But I try to push Ava out of my mind for now to concentrate on Zelda.

"I want to take you to my tree house," she says. "It's where I was going with all those books when I dropped them at your feet."

It's a reassuring offer, because it shows that she trusts me. And isn't it about time?

On our way, we stop for a moment of reflection on our bridge.

"That day we met doesn't seem so long ago, does it?" The ducks quack at her for crackers, but she makes a show of her empty palms.

"It wasn't that long ago." I scrounge for a stale cracker in the pocket of my sport coat and give it to her to appease the ducks. "But I still feel like I've known you forever."

"I'm so happy I've gotten the chance to know you." She retrieves a pocket knife from one of her ankle boots and carves

$Z + R$ into the wood. It's a surprising and flattering gesture. Even though I know it's shown up in hundreds of Novels, in this moment it feels unique.

She takes my hand, and we walk on with our fingers entwined. Maybe this talk will turn out well, after all.

Her tree house hides itself well in plain sight. She has to point it out to me before I can find it in the canopy of leaves above us. She sheds her gold snowsuit bottoms to reveal a simple pair of black leggings underneath.

"Watch your head," she warns as we climb the wooden slats nailed to the trunk. "The ceiling hangs low."

Once inside, I whistle. "Wow. You have a lot of treasures, don't you?"

The floor of the tree house sags with clutter. In one corner lies a croquet mallet next to a yellow blow-up chair that, thanks to algae stains, looks like it was rescued from the neglected life of a pool floatie. A makeshift bookcase supports a vintage set of encyclopedias, a pair of binoculars, and a dog-eared guide to the birds of North America. And a tray table holds a microscope with an assortment of marked slides and glass beakers and other science-y stuff.

"Thank you for not calling it junk." She clears a space for me on a braided rag rug and I sit across from her.

"Anything for you, Empress of the Anatidae."

"Riley." Her eyes are wet and sad. She gives me this uncomfortable sort of smile that tells me she's about to say something she knows I won't want to hear.

So I cover my ears. "Don't."

She reaches up and removes my hands and puts them back in my lap. "I've been thinking it over, and this whole Pixie-Off plan is simply too risky for me. I've decided my best option is to plant."

I'm stunned. "But we *dazzled* Bridget. We can do this, I know we can." I have to believe that, because *I* don't have the option of planting.

"Riley." She sniffles. This is as difficult for her as it is for me, which is some consolation. "If only you could plant with me."

When I don't answer, she babbles on. "Though I guess that would be awkward because Chet and my character in the book have a happy ending. But that's a moot point since you can't plant in a book you never worked on."

Hearing Chet's name is like a thousand porcupine quills straight in the heart. "You get a happy ending?"

She smiles sadly. "Isn't a happy ending what we always say we want?"

"But that's not *your* happy ending. That's a character called Priscilla's happy ending. Will you be content with playing out a character all your life?"

"It's better than being retired."

"The Council may still decide to keep us on." Depending on whether we go through with the plan to sabotage Nebraska . . .

"For now, maybe. But do you really want that axe hanging over your head?"

"Well . . ." I take a deep breath. "If the Council's decision doesn't go the way we hope, there's still another option. What if Finn was right? What if the Termination Train isn't an ending, but a new beginning?"

"It's a fantasy," she says firmly. "Born out of desperation and deception. That's all it is."

"Let's work this out logically," I propose, realizing as the words come out of my mouth that logic is not something Manic Pixies are especially known for. "What we *do* know is outdated Tropes are retired to the Trope Museum, right?"

"We saw that with our own eyes." Zelda shudders.

"But why would the Council bother with all that if they had a much easier and faster method like the train?"

Zelda shrugs. "Okay, let's say your hunch is right, and we do make it to Reader World. What then? What if our Trope brains are too limited to handle all the infinite possibilities of a self-controlled life?"

"I believe we're capable of growing—capable of dealing with a more complex universe," I say. "You yearn for freedom the same as I do. Otherwise you wouldn't have risked going Off-Page for that rumor."

"I do," she says carefully. She scrunches up her mouth, as if possibly reconsidering. It gives me hope.

"I know it's a risk, but it's a chance to live life according to our own rules." I smack my palms so hard on the floor that the glass slides rattle. "It's the only opportunity we'll ever have to write our own stories."

She shakes her head. "I wish I were as brave as you are."

"You are braver by far," I insist. "Please stay with me. We can face whatever comes together."

"I love that you're idealistic and romantic, but we need to be pragmatic. We are talking life and death stakes here. If our roles were reversed, I would be begging you to plant." The urgency in her voice reveals her fear, but also how much she truly cares about me.

Am I being selfish to ask her to throw away her one sure avenue for continued existence? Maybe I am. If she plants, at least one of us will be guaranteed to survive.

"You're right," I say, even though a part of me dies when I say it.

She touches a finger to my lips. "I've already decided. I'll plant tomorrow afternoon during my final work session. My Novel is nearly done."

"But that means . . ."

"I won't be there for the Pixie-Off."

After all we've been through in the name of seeking justice for our Trope, she's not even going to stay to see our defense through. A direct punch to my kidney would hurt less.

"I know it sucks," she says in the understatement of the year, "but it's my last window to plant. And you don't need me."

If she only knew how much I needed her. But telling her that won't change anything. Even if there's no happy end in the cards for me, I can be happy for hers. "I'll miss you."

"Hey! This isn't goodbye!"

"It isn't?" Hope swells up my chest.

"Come over to my apartment tomorrow morning. I want to give you something before I go."

And hope leaves again in my next heavy exhale.

I have the urge to scream in frustration at the universe introducing us, showing me how amazing life can be, and then taking her away. I know it's the typical character arc of the Manic Pixie Dream Girl, but this time is more agonizing because it's happening to me. "Okay. See you tomorrow."

Still sitting, she leans forward and gives me an awkward hug that's all arms. "See you."

On my walk home, I go the long way around the park so I can avoid our bridge and our initials. All they are now is a permanent monument to my heartbreak.

Ava sneaks into my mind again. My belief in her led her to take a giant risk in leaving her novel. And her belief in me may be what saves our Trope from extinction. Don't I believe in myself enough to give myself the chance to make my own adventures, too?

When I get home, I sit and face my heart mosaic hanging on the wall. I remember how Clark mourned the loss of his perfectly formed glass lobsters. Maybe I'm like one of those glass lobsters: if I can break out of my restricting mold, I can put the pieces of myself back together in a way that reflects who I've grown to be. It might be messier, but it'll be all mine.

The more I think about everything, the more convinced I am that the Termination Train is truly is the gateway to Reader World. I decide that I am going to go, whether or not the Pixie-Off saves our Trope. With or without Zelda.

Because I owe it to myself to be my authentic self.

CHAPTER 58

The first time I visit Zelda's apartment, it doesn't feel like it's hers. Her personality is packed away, with all her comic books stacked in cardboard boxes, her posters fitted snugly into tubes, and her boho furniture wrapped in sheets of plastic. She's even reverted the walls to their standard white, though she's done a sloppy job because I can still make out slivers of yellow paint along the baseboards and near the ceiling. I also detect a few dried spaghetti stragglers hanging on for dear life over her stove, and they make me nostalgic for Zelda's spunk in the early days of our acquaintance.

"I don't even know why I bothered packing." She hands me a broom and a dustpan. "Except that the Council told me to, and I'm ultimately accommodating, apparently."

I sweep the wood floor in the living room while she mops the kitchen. I collect the detritus of her life here in my dustpan: graham cracker crumbs, sea green sequins, and torn-up bits of construction paper. I also find one of her silver buttons, Hg-80, otherwise known as mercury, one of the most toxic elements on the periodic table. It's so strong it has the power to dissolve gold and silver.

The pin begs me to crush it under my foot. A metaphorical

stamping out of the choice she's making. But if I do that, I'm part of the problem. I'd be another loser guy who thinks of her only as a shiny concept and not as a real person with complicated constellations inside her.

So I pick it up delicately and set it on her empty table. She can decide what to do with it.

When she finishes in the kitchen, she takes the full dustpan from me. She raises an eyebrow when she sees the button lying forlornly on the table, but she doesn't comment. She empties the dustpan into a trash bag, wipes off her hands on her jeans, and goes over to a box and digs around in it.

She pulls out a container with her button-making machine and supplies, all neatly organized, and hands it to me. "I wanted you to have this. I know you'll appreciate it."

I hug it to my chest and will myself not to cry. I don't want her last memory of me to be tearstained. "Will I see you again?" I ask, though the chances are slim to absolute zero.

"You never know." She pushes me against a wall.

And she kisses me. On the mouth. And the universe spins like it might explode from the sheer awesomeness of it.

I slip my hands around her waist and pull her closer to me, and we allow our bodies to communicate all the feelings our minds never found the right words for.

Why does our first kiss also have to be our last?

If I don't open my eyes, can I stay in the moment forever?

"Don't forget this." Zelda slips away from me.

"Like I ever could." I think she means the kiss. But when I finally open my eyes, she holds out the button-making kit.

"Goodbye, Riley. And good luck in the Pixie-Off and beyond."

I'm so choked up at this point, I can't even speak. So I

merely take the kit from her. I blow her a half kiss and walk out her door and out of her story.

On her doorstep, I get a last-ditch idea. I take out one of the silver pieces of cardstock and a black marker. I form ZE in large block letters, but instead of a number, I write: "Be your own element."

I stamp all it together in the machine and leave the button on her doormat.

CHAPTER 59

The green room behind the Town Hall auditorium hosts a full-on Pixie Panic. With Zelda out, all the pressure falls on the remaining six of us. And without Angela to help us focus our scattered energy, we're fractious and flighty.

Our de-facto dictator primps in the mirror with a treacherous mascara wand. "Pink glitter clumps will be the death of me," Nebraska wails.

Nebraska is not one to lose her cool, so her outburst adds to the tension. Chloe dissolves into tears. Sky pats her back like she's playing a set of bongos, which might make Chloe laugh in less stressful times, but only succeeds in making her cry harder.

George is sulking because she hasn't been able to find Angela, and no one has any idea where she is.

Mandy pays too much attention to the drama and not enough to her curling iron and soon enough it stinks of rotting eggs.

"Mandy!" I snap my fingers in front of her. "Your hair!"

A big chunk of blond falls to the floor, leaving singed tendrils over her right ear. "What the felt!" She flings the iron down in horror.

Personally, I play a loop in my head of Zelda running

and jumping into Chet's waiting arms, probably at this very moment. Each replay makes me more despondent. I also haven't seen or heard from Ava since Bridget escorted her away. Maybe the Council decided she's a rabble-rouser and condemned her to the VZ. She's completely at their mercy.

In short, we are not even remotely in the mood to scamper around the stage showing off our best sides for the Council.

Chloe blows her nose on the first flowing fabric she can find, which happens to be the chiffon train of Nebraska's miniskirt ball gown.

Nebraska's gasp echoes through the room, and you could easily hear one of Mandy's bobby pins drop while we wait for a further reaction.

Instead, we hear a knock on the door.

I open it, and Angela slips in, but not before looking both ways down the hall, as if she worries that the Council might prevent her visit.

The relief in the room is palpable, and George throws herself into Angela's arms. I turn away to give them some privacy.

"Hi girls. And Riley." Angela does her jazz hands greeting, just like old times. "Sorry I haven't had time to check in. My new assignment is with the Sensitive Nice Guy Trope, and their sessions go on *forever.*" Having had Clark nearly take up permanent residence on my sofa, I can sympathize.

With her and George's permission, we pile on Angela like she's scored the winning touchdown. Obviously we've missed her, too. And we could sure as felt use a pep talk about now.

Angela senses this, of course, and lines us up in a row, surveying us with her therapist eye. "You know what's at stake here," she admonishes softly. "This is not the time to fall apart. So if you can't help but fall, your best bet is to fall together."

"What do you mean?" Mandy asks.

"She means we need to support each other," I say, looking meaningfully at each of Nebraska's potential saboteurs.

Sky clears her throat. "I wrote a song with Nebraska for her to sing solo, but I think we should all sing it."

Sky is on to something. After all, what seems like bragging when an individual does it might be interpreted as confidence when a group does.

"That's brilliant!" I throw in my support. Everyone but Nebraska murmurs her assent.

"Nebraska?" Sky asks tentatively.

There is a collective intake of breath as we wait for Nebraska's opinion on the matter.

"Yes." She takes a pair of scissors and cuts the ruined train from her dress. "Let's do that."

We gather around the lyrics sheet that Sky wrote out. It's hilariously over-the-top, and I have to clamp my jaw to keep from laughing.

Ode to Me

I'm a Manic Pixie Dream Girl
Go on, give me a whirl
Gorgeous as the month of May
I make your troubles seem far away

I bake sparkles in cream pie
Tattooed a unicorn on my thigh
Witty, wise, and down to skate
I really am the perfect date

Never dull, always fun
I skip and dance but seldom run
Sing along and you will see
Every day's a plus with me

"Okay," Angela says diplomatically. "For it to work for the whole group, you're going to have to revise to include Riley."

We throw out a flurry of suggestions, crossing out lines and adding others until we are satisfied we've brought the requisite awesome. Sky pulls out her guitar and strums the music part for us. Fortunately, she's much more talented at it than I am.

And as we're rehearsing, it becomes clear that the focus of the song has shifted—in a way that's deeper than a switch from singular to plural. I'm increasingly amped up for the opportunity to get out there and share this.

Nebraska watches us silently until we're done. At last, she reasserts her leadership role: "Individuals who contribute to a whole. That's who we are. We'll sing the first and last verses together, and in between, break out. Do our own thing. Mandy, you'll be up first."

There's another knock on the door. Angela opens it without hesitation.

Bridget is outside. She raises an eyebrow. "It's time."

CHAPTER 60

We file out and head toward the stage. Angela takes a seat in the audience and doesn't even glance in the Council's direction. She's here for us.

The other 150 Manic Pixies shout out support. They wave homemade banners brimming with positive mantras.

We face the Council, waiting for the green light.

Bridget nods. "Proceed."

Chloe, Mandy, and George mount the stage with clumsy cartwheels as Sky and I lift Nebraska, and she performs an elegant back handspring from our upraised palms. I raise Sky and her guitar into position and spring up to join my friends and frenemy.

> *We're not your concept*
> *We're not here to be your toy*
> *We have rich inner lives*
> *All these girls and this one boy . . .*

Thanks to our last-minute revisions, we're no longer defending our right to continue existing as one-dimensional bundles of quirk. We're asserting our capacity to be multifaceted, deeper versions of ourselves. Maybe we'll never be as complicated as Developeds, but we don't have to be as flat as microfilm either.

Mandy uses her baby-doll cuteness to her advantage. She skitters to the front of the stage and sings a cappella in a breathy voice. Chloe interprets Mandy's words with dramatic body movements and silver streamers.

Once I thought I had to give it all
and accept nothing in return
but gratitude for a job well done

Now I follow my own star
And if he wants to come along
He has to bring at least half the fun

Angela claps from the front row with a huge smile on her face, which emboldens Sky to come out head-banging with her guitar. She doesn't sing, but she speaks joyfully via the music. It strips away my worries and encourages me to live my best life, no matter what. I do a running leap and slide forward on the stage on my knees. It's a move that looks cool, but it probably also rips off the top layer of skin. It's worth it for the cheers that erupt behind me.

We clear the way for George, who gives an abridged encore performance of her tap dance that broke us out of jail. As she taps her shoes against the stage (*spank* HEEL *shuffle* HEEL *step*), she composes a slam poem on the fly.

Confined. Far too long.
Defined. By your expectations.

Refined. By your exhortations.
Now I'm free.
I'm not the girl in the box I used to be.
You can love me or you can ignore me.
Doesn't matter, I'm still me.

She ends with a shiggy bop, and a curtsy. The rest of us attempt our own shiggy bops, with varying degrees of executional success.

Next each of the girls spins me in turn until I'm dizzy enough to believe Zelda is bounding toward me, even though that can't possibly be true because she's light-years gone by now. Unreachable.

There's a popping sound, followed by a burst of yellow smoke and falling gold glitter. I close my eyes and let it cleanse my soul. When I open my eyes, the smoke has cleared and Zelda winks at me, resplendent in a silver bodysuit with the letters ZE painted across the chest.

She leans over and whispers into my ear, "I finally found my element."

I feel like I'm having the happy kind of heart attack. The kind that alerts you in blaring, bleating throbs that you're still alive and life is freaking amazing.

I kiss her for courage and begin to belt out our final verse. The other girls sing in harmony, and we link arms across the stage.

Our manic energy lights up the world
When our pixie charm unfurls
Don't let us become a forgotten dream
Cuz we jazz up reality

But of course, Nebraska can't leave it at that, so after we take our triumphant joint bow, she adds her own coda.

Sing along and you will see
Every day's a plus with . . .

We all expect her final word to be "me", and she drags out the "with" extra long, raising the suspense. But when it finally comes, her last word is . . .

us!

It may be the sweetest word I've ever heard.

The Council rewards us with a standing ovation, and once all our celebrating winds down, Bridget approaches Nebraska and shakes her hand. Her fussiness has melted away and she actually kicks up her feet in something resembling a jig. If *that* doesn't make you believe in Manic Pixie magic, nothing will.

"Congratulations," Bridget trills. "In a unanimous, spontaneous decision, we have decided to let your Trope continue. May you spread joy wherever you go."

A blur of hugs and happy tears follows. The Council begins distributing balloons, and the multitude of Manic Pixies comes to blow them up with abandon. Where there are balloons, there is also popping, and because I'm well aware from her character trait sheet that balloon popping is Zelda's Achilles' heel, I whisk her away to the green room. There will be time enough later to party with my fellow Pixies.

CHAPTER 61

When we're alone in the green room, Zelda kisses me again. It's not the goodbye kiss of yesterday, it's the hello kiss of the future. I want to get lost in it, but I can't. Because I'm thinking about Ava.

"Something wrong?" Zelda breaks only a sliver away so that she murmurs her question into my mouth. It's crazy sexy, but I force myself to put some distance between us.

"Ummm . . . I'm not sure how to put this . . ."

"You're in love with Ava," she states. She doesn't look upset about it though, just thoughtful.

"I don't know." Where I feel fluttery and euphoric around Zelda, I feel cozy and carefree around Ava. "There's so much going on right now, and I guess I need some time to process it all."

Zelda winks and slugs me tenderly in the shoulder. "Same. No need to rush into anything. I want the space to figure out who I am beyond the label I've been given."

The door flings open. "Oh," Nebraska says innocently. "Am I interrupting a *private* moment?" Ava stands beside her, looking a little bit lost.

"Not at all," Zelda says without a trace of malice. "Come on in, Ava. It's so awesome to finally meet you."

Ava beams at her and approaches us with pep in her step. "Thank you. It's been a whirlwind couple of days, hasn't it?"

She turns to me with her goofy grin, and I envelop her in my arms. It feels so right to have her back in my life.

Nebraska wrinkles her nose. "Indeed. Bridget thought I should bid you farewell before I go, so here I am."

Wait. Nebraska is leaving? A wild thought occurs to me. "Are you taking the Termination Train after all? To Reader World?"

"Still on that kick, are you? I already told you—I'm not interested in putting myself at the mercy of reality."

Zelda's eyebrows scrunch together as she looks back and forth between Nebraska and me. "Riley, even if the train really does lead to Reader World . . ."

"It does," Nebraska interrupts.

Zelda pauses and repeats, "If it does . . ."

"What?" Nebraska protests. "I have no reason to lie to you now."

Zelda continues. "Now that our Trope has been saved, there's no longer any pressure on us to risk so much."

"And Bridget is offering everyone in our therapy group promotions to Legacy and big houses in TropeTown Heights," Nebraska singsongs. "The others already accepted."

Legacy. A big house. It sounds like a dream.

But it's not my dream. And now that I know Reader World is within my grasp, I could never be satisfied living out other people's stories. No way.

"I'm taking the train," I declare with all the confidence I have stored up. "Because my destiny is to embrace possibility."

"Mine, too," Ava says. I expected nothing less of her.

I turn to Zelda, and so many of our times together flash through my mind. Stargazing at Winter Lake. Going Off-Page.

Breaking out of Jail. Being with her may not turn out to be my destiny after all, but I'm not ready to rule it out yet. "And you?" I ask her.

"I'm taking the train, too," Zelda says. "Because even if it ultimately turns out to be short-lived, it will be an adventure I choose."

"Whatever." Nebraska slicks her jagged hair back into a sleek bun. "As a reward for practically *singlehandedly* saving the Trope, the Council granted me a transfer to Mean Girl Mastermind, so I don't really care what all you Manic Pixies do now."

"So you confessed to the arson!" Zelda exclaims. To be transferred to a villain role, Nebraska would've had to confess to committing a crime.

"I did indeed," Nebraska confirms. "Georgina's name is officially cleared. That's something else you can thank me for."

Of course we know that justice for George wasn't her motivation, but I'm still immensely relieved for George's sake. And Mean Girl Mastermind is a perfect fit for a devious egomaniac like Nebraska.

As she turns to leave, she says, "You can do me one favor, though. When you see Finn, tell him I'm sorry."

CHAPTER 62

Before we go, I have to tie up some loose ends—namely, a dozen newly formed Manic Pixie Dream Boys sitting in the front two rows of Town Hall auditorium. They squint at me as though I know the secrets of the universe.

And heck, maybe I do. But I learned them the hard way, and they'll have to, too. Wisdom does not come for free, my friends.

Angela stands next to me. She's been reassigned again—at her request—to be responsible for their twelve-week orientation, and she seems genuinely excited for the challenge.

"I was so upset on my first day with Angela," I admit to the room. "I thought being assigned to group therapy was a punishment—that it meant I was a failure. But it turned out to be a huge gift. It gave me a loyal circle of friends, confidence in myself, and a bright future."

Angela pats me on the back. "I'm so proud of who you've become," she says, choking me up even more.

I wipe a tear from my eye and continue. "You all are going to sweep into a bunch of different characters' lives and mess up all their plans in order to give them the gift of possibility," I tell them. I wink at Zelda and Ava, who both wait in the wings for me.

"That's right," Angela says, summoning George over and putting her arm around her. "And one day, if you're lucky like I am, you'll find the girl who sticks around and joins you on this great adventure called life."

The new boys whoop in appreciation for our joint inspirational speech. I salute the new recruits and give Angela and George goodbye bear hugs. Zelda, Ava, and I have a train to catch.

Mandy, Chloe, and Sky come to see us off at the station. We say tearful goodbyes to our dear friends and board the train.

CHAPTER 63

As the train pulls around the curve into the station, I take in the gleaming terra-cotta bricks on the domed ceiling of the tunnel. Soft yellow light streams down from the stained-glass skylights and brass chandeliers, illuminating the passage like a vintage filter might. We come to a halt right in front of an arched stairwell leading up. The plaque proclaims this gorgeous place as City Hall.

The doors of our train creak open, and Ava, Zelda, and I exchange befuddled glances. What does it mean that the station is completely deserted? Have we been sent to a whimsical afterlife—forever fated to wander picturesque tunnels in the belly of the Earth?

The conductor blows a whistle. "This is the termination of your journey. Please watch your step as you exit the train."

Termination Train.

The gap between the platform and us looms unnervingly wide and steep. But we all three join hands and take the daring leap.

When we hit the smooth surface of the landing, a muffled meow rumbles my backpack. I unzip my bag, and Sprite comes tumbling out.

"Silly kitty," I scold. "Cathy will miss you."

Sprite rubs against my legs, furring up my jeans in the process—and who knows how long I'll have to wear these. She stands on her hind legs and paws at my knees for me to pick her up. "Fine. I'm glad you're here, okay?"

She purrs when I cradle her against my chest. Zelda scratches her behind the ears with a silly grin on her face.

The train pulls away, and we stand and listen until the last echoes of its departure have faded.

"So what do we do now?" Ava asks.

"We climb out into the unknown and see where life takes us," I say, sounding more confident than I actually feel.

Zelda bounces on her heels. "I'm ready!"

A figure stands at the top of the stairs, in shadow, but when he descends toward us, I recognize Finn's wavy hair and pinstripes. His eyebrows rise when he sees it's me without Nebraska, but he bounds over with a huge smile.

"Riley! You finally made it!"

"Is this Reader World?" I ask, all my hopes knotted in my throat.

Finn's grin widens. "Welcome to New York City."

EPILOGUE

So there you go. I wrote my story. And I am still writing it. Every single day.

Are you ready to write yours?

ACKNOWLEDGMENTS

"Can you think of any examples of Manic Pixie Dream *Boys*?" This was the question—posed by my transformative second-semester advisor, Susan Fletcher—that birthed Riley and TropeTown during my MFA program at Vermont College of Fine Arts. I am deeply grateful to my classmates and advisors at VCFA for showing such enthusiasm for the project: to my advisors Louise Hawes and Shelley Tanaka for your mentorship, to Kekla Magoon and Mark Karlin's workshop for your invaluable early feedback, to my fourth-semester advisor, William Alexander, for spurring me on to great quirky heights and meaningful depths as TropeTown developed into my creative thesis, and to everyone (especially my fellow ThemePunks) who came out for my grad reading, Riley's first public outing.

Riley matured even further to become the delightfully complex MANic Pixie he is today thanks to the salesmanship and support of Legacy super-agent Stephen Barbara and the awesome, AU-worthy insight of editor Amy Fitzgerald. Jazz hands and glitter go out to book designer Emily Harris and my beta readers: Ann Bonwill, Christina Franke, Robin Galbraith, David Hoffman, and Yamile Saied Mendez. And finally, a heartfelt aria of gratitude to my biggest Off-Page fans: my husband Michael and my family.

Riley's journey from playing a prescribed role to embracing his authentic self and stepping up to become the hero of his own story somewhat mirrors the process I went through myself during the conception and writing of this novel. I hope it inspires you, too, to reject the labels others may bestow upon you and instead define yourself on your own terms. Always remember: you have the power to write your own life.

TOPICS FOR DISCUSSION

1. Why is Riley so fascinated by Zelda? What sets her apart from the Manic Pixies he meets?

2. In TropeTown, Manic Pixies can be terminated if they don't fulfill the roles that authors write for them. What are the pros and cons of playing the role that they are programmed to play?

3. Riley admits to himself that he doesn't really know what love is. To what extent do you think his feelings for Zelda are about who she is, and to what extent are they caused by his programming?

4. Riley struggles to give Clark relationship advice. Why does he have trouble deciding what to say? How is this encounter different from the kinds of interactions he's used to?

5. Do you think Ava and other Developeds are better off than the Tropes? How much of her life and personality are controlled by the Author? In what ways does she grow beyond the Author's original intent? Riley is concerned that playing the same character like the Manic Pixie Dream Boy over and over again will result in him becoming a watered-down or embittered version of himself. In what ways can this happen to teens in real life?

6. George is frustrated that her roles only seem to exist to shake up the lives of main characters who are almost always white guys. Angela frames this as a privilege and a way to make a difference. In what ways can the Tropes make a positive impact on Developeds and, by extension, on Readers? In what ways could their roles have a negative effect?

7. Why do you think Nebraska became so cynical and manipulative?

8. What are the differences between TropeTown and the real world? As Riley sees it, what are the advantages of Reader World? What does TropeTown offer its residents that Reader World doesn't?

9. Why does Riley decide not to plant in his novel? What does this choice say about his values and his goals?

10. At the Trope Museum, Riley becomes concerned that his existence supports problematic stereotypes. In what ways have stereotypical characters like the ones in the museum harmed Readers and society at large? What do you think is an appropriate way for Riley to respond to his Trope's problematic legacy?

11. What arguments do the Manic Pixies make in their defense at the Council hearing? How is the message of their Pixie-Off performance different from the message of Nebraska's speech?

12. When Riley decides to board the train, he is risking his life for the chance to have free will. What responsibilities will come with that freedom? How do you think he will cope with the challenges of life in Reader World?

ABOUT THE AUTHOR

Lenore Appelhans is the author of several books for children and teens. Her work has appeared on the Bank Street Best Books list, won a SCBWI Crystal Kite award, and been featured on boxes of Cheerios. Lenore is an ambivert, a proud Slytherpuff, and a world traveler. She holds an MFA in Creative Writing from Vermont College of Fine Arts. She lives in the D.C. area with her family and her manic pixie dream cat.